SCHOLASTIC

Workshops That Work

30 Days of Mini-Lessons That Help Launch and Establish All Important Routines for an Effective Reading and Writing Workshop

by Kirsten Widmer & Sarah Buxton

New York • Toronto • London • Auckland • Sydney
Mexico City • New Delhi • Hong Kong • Buenos Aires

Teaching Resources

Dedication

For my mother, my first teacher.
—SB

Cover design by Jaime Lucero
Interior design by LDL Designs
Cover photo James Levin
Interior photos courtesy of authors

ISBN 0-439-44406-3

Printed in the U.S.A.
4 5 6 7 8 9 10 23 09 08 07 06

Table of Contents

Preface

A Place to Begin... Two years ago, we were asked to create a launching unit for new literacy teachers in our district. We wrote a study because we realized there were many, many new teachers who needed a place to begin in September. While we strongly believe that working with a staff developer is the most effective means of learning the workshop model, we know that most professional opportunities do not surface until mid-September, often late October, while some districts are not even able to provide such costly programs.

Our launching unit was met with open arms by many of the teachers from our district. Here are our lessons. They are a place to begin—by no means all that one needs to know about teaching Reading and Writing Workshop, but a good foundation to build upon.

How to Use These Lessons

There are many amazing resources for learning about the Reading and Writing Workshop. There are books about craft studies, books that focus on each part of the workshop (such as the mini-lesson and the conference), books that explore reading and writing strategies, and books that share teaching philosophies. There are also books that contain lesson plans for teachers. This is one of those books.

And it is not.

The philosophy behind Reading and Writing Workshop holds that teachers must be reactive and teach according to the needs of their students. This conviction guides all of the teaching we do. While writing this book, of course, we couldn't react to the needs of students we'd never met, who go to schools we've never visited; we were concerned about writing lessons for students we didn't know. So we shared lessons that were successful in setting up the workshop in our classrooms and, out of these, created blanket lessons. We wrote as though we were teaching our classes. We envisioned our students as we wrote to yours.

Our aim was to provide a teacher who is new to Reading and Writing Workshop with a basis for beginning. We have tried to show you the planning that goes into launching a successful workshop and also give you the language for doing so. We have tried to give you a sense of what the workshop sounds and looks like in action. These lessons will help guide you in the right direction. The Reading and Writing Workshop is layered; it is full of possibilities. We have only touched upon the very outer layer of this type of teaching.

From our own experience, we know that no book can replace the work of a staff developer. We suggest that you use these lessons to begin discussions with staff developers and colleagues in your school or district. We also recommend reading from the list of professional books that we have included.

Pacing the Lessons

While we have provided lessons for the first thirty days of school, we by no means assume it will only take you thirty days to implement them. Be responsive to the needs of your students. If they need you to spend more time on any given mini-lesson, then do so. There are many lessons included in the study that could be fleshed out over two or three days; we include ideas for extending these lessons in the follow-up sections.

You decide how you will structure the workshops over the week. Some teachers, especially in schools that use block scheduling (two 45-minute periods in a row), choose to have each workshop last 90 minutes and to alternate reading and writing workshop each day. Other teachers on block scheduling have included reading and writing each day by opting for a system of "majors" and "minors." On a given day, the major workshop would last for 60 minutes and be followed by a minor workshop of 30 minutes. The minor workshop usually includes a quick follow-up mini-lesson, followed by independent work, conferring, and sharing. Still other teachers split their block evenly, using 45 minutes for each workshop each day. Others not on block schedule alternate 45-minute workshops over the course of the week. No matter what schedule you choose, we highly recommend implementing the reading lessons and the writing lessons in the order they appear in the book. We don't suggest that you pick and choose lessons by title. The launching unit of study is focused on the idea that there is a process to learning. As the lessons move forward, students move forward in the process of thinking and writing and reading. Each lesson, both in reading and writing, builds upon and makes connections to the last. However, based on your own assessments and knowledge of the students you teach, you may find that some of the lessons don't fit your needs closely enough. If so, use the lessons as templates for creating your own.

Lesson Layout and Components

The lessons are written in two font styles—regular and italics. Where the style is regular, we are providing a model of language for you to use with your students. This language is meant to give you a way of "hearing" what a lesson might sound like as it unfolds. Some of this language isn't in complete sentences, or it may seem unrefined; it's meant to represent dialogue. We attempted to capture the way we speak in front of a class, and you will see a difference between our writing here and in the regular font in the lessons.

Where the style is italics, we are speaking directly to you, the teacher. We offer suggestions about what to look for when students are working independently or what you might ask students during conferences. We also show you how to prepare for and carry out each lesson.

Essential to the workshop is your ability to model your own work and thought processes. You will find that the success of the lessons depends on your ability to show your students how you yourself read, write, think, and learn. For instance, listing the steps it takes to write a draft is not nearly as effective as modeling how to make a draft, and then recapping the steps as you summarize them in a chart with students.

As you read through these lessons, notice that we share our personal stories with our students. We do this to model good writing and reading practices as well as to build a sense of community within the classroom. We encourage you to launch your own conversations and personal storytelling with your classes.

We have included excerpts from our journals and snippets of conversations with students in order to give you insight into what has happened in our classrooms. What happens in your classroom will be similar but will sound and flow a bit differently. No two writing workshops are ever the same. Every member of the writing and reading community, teacher and student alike, brings to the workshop a different personality and unique set of stories to share.

How Workshop Lessons Change Over the Year

The first few weeks are the most important in the year. During this time, you will establish the rules, structures, and expectations that allow you to teach effectively. The entire workshop depends upon smooth transitions, quiet independent and conference times, and the ability of students to stay on task and have conversations with peers. The lessons in this book will help you establish the structure you need.

Your teaching will begin to be shaped by whole-class discussions and individual conferences you have with your students. As the year moves on and students become familiar with the structures and rituals of the workshop, they will speak about reading and writing with greater sophistication, and you will have opportunities to teach finer and more complicated ideas. As the classroom community becomes closely knit, the conversation about writing will intensify, written work will strengthen, and a passion for books will bloom.

Workshop Essentials

This next section provides an overview of some essential workshop elements: assessment, which gives you a baseline for instruction; workshop format, a guide to the structure of a typical workshop session; the classroom environment, which outlines some ideas for arranging furniture and materials to support workshop activities; and finally, charts, which record the learning and become invaluable reference tools.

Assessment

Assessment is essential to the teaching of Reading and Writing Workshop. It's the way that you, as a teacher, gather information about your students—what they already know, what you need to teach them, and how well you've taught them. It's also the way that students begin to see their progress and come to understand that it's our job, as teachers, to know what they are doing in order to teach them to be better readers and writers. By assessing students, we make clear our thinking and our goals not only to them but also to ourselves. This serves as the backbone for our work and planning.

Assessing for Reading Workshop

Early in the year, assessment gives us a clearer picture of our students as readers. This doesn't mean that we look only at their standardized reading test scores. We need to provide our students with authentic ways to show us who they are as readers. We need to act as researchers in our classrooms, compiling enough information about our students' reading lives to give us ideas about how far they've come as reader, and where we might be able to take them.

For the purposes of launching Reading Workshop, the major goal of assessment is to gain a sense of each student's independent reading level. Independent reading is meant to be easy for students—they shouldn't struggle with words, concepts, or content. Independent reading books—"just-right" books—are those books students can read on their own without needing a teacher's direct intervention or support. In other words, while you may confer with students and support their efforts to notice and use certain reading or comprehension strategies, your support shouldn't be *necessary* for students to understand what they are reading. We need to have a clear picture of students' independent reading levels in order to support them in making good choices about books. This is especially important in classrooms with struggling readers.

In our first year of teaching, we noticed that many of our students had already had terrible experiences with reading—they couldn't name a book they had read recently or even a book they liked. Many of them had no idea of what reading a "just-right" book felt like. For them, reading had always been difficult, and they got through classes either by pretending to read, by refusing to read because "it's boring," or by being consistent behavior problems—they'd get kicked out of the classroom, so they wouldn't have to read any more.

We found that assessing these students early gave us time not only to support them as readers but also to gain their trust as teachers of reading. It gave us time to provide them with positive reading experiences through shared reading and read aloud. It also gave us time to have honest conversations with them about their reluctance to read, what it meant, and what it would mean for them to become better readers. By addressing our students' reading issues and providing the specific support they needed, we helped them make great strides in their attitudes toward reading and in their abilities to read and comprehend. We would not have been able to do this without first assessing them.

In the urban schools we taught in, where reading test scores are generally low, the majority of our students were reading at least two levels below grade. Most of our seventh graders, for example, could comfortably read and understand a fifth grade text. In time, we were able to accurately assess students' reading using their chosen books, but at the beginning of the year we used the same text with all students. Seeing how each student understood the same text made clear what kinds of mini-lessons we needed to teach in order to support comprehension, word attack skills, and appropriate text choice.

Here are the steps we took that worked well in assessing students:

- We selected a text that was two grade levels below where our students were supposed to be reading. (Our staff developers recommended a book with a grade level on the back, but these numbers can be inaccurate, so you should investigate the level for yourself.) There is also a variety of different leveling systems available. You might want to check with your district or school about the leveling system they use or might want to adopt. Some books about the subject we've found helpful: Fountas & Pinnell's *Guiding Readers and Writers 3–6* and Lucy Calkins' *A Field Guide to the Classroom Library*.
- We made multiple photocopies of a passage from the book for ourselves, to use as a running record of each students' skills, and gave copies of the book to our students.
- We asked students to look over the first page or so of the text—to read it silently, get acquainted with it. Then we asked them to read the text aloud to us. On our photocopied sheets, we noted where a student stumbled, went back and self-corrected, or substituted one word for another (we wrote their word over the word used in the text). We noted whether the student read with inflection, followed punctuation, or used his finger to mark his place. Also, we tried to notice if a student tried out words under her breath before saying them, and took note of whether a student asked for help.
- Then we asked the student to retell the reading. On the back of our photocopy, we tried to write exactly what the student said (sometimes this was rough if the student was a fast talker, but we did our best!). We were careful to note if a student looked back at the story for names (a good strategy), or if she simply reread sentences. If a student said, "I don't know," we asked specific questions about the passage to see what the student did comprehend.
- After thinking about all the information we received, we assessed our students to determine if they needed to read texts at the level of the assessment, at a lower level, or at a higher one. A student who read fluently and whose retelling showed a clear grasp of the text—for instance, the student accurately summarized the dialogue—is probably ready for a higher-level text. In all cases, we discussed our findings with our students individually and talked about their book choices.

While we found this process to be somewhat time-consuming at first, we managed to assess our entire class in a few weeks. It was an invaluable practice for us. Typically, in order to get a sense of a child's reading, you need to have them read about 150 to 200 words of text. For your running record, only make a copy of the section of text you plan for the students to read aloud. That way, you can mark it up with their miscues, and make notes on their fluency and comprehension on the text itself. The text you give the child should be something that makes sense—where you don't need to give background, explain characters, etc. It should be something that students can easily retell. You can also quickly assess students' levels and book choices by having them go through a similar process with their own independent reading books. (Obviously you won't be able to photocopy a page of everyone's book, but you can just take note of word substitutions, stumblings, and so on in your conferring notes.) If you're not confident in your assessments, you can always check yourself by giving a student what you believe is a "just-right" book and asking him to read parts of it to you, noting his degree of fluency and comprehension.

In the end, the assessments save time because they let you know where to begin your teaching and your conferring. And it gives you a good idea of how to stock your library. If you are given a classroom library full of sixth-grade level texts, and you discover that most of your students comfortably read fourth-grade level books, you're going to need to find some fourth-grade level books for your library. Otherwise your students will struggle with reading all year long. Understanding your students' strengths and weaknesses—individually and as a class—is a key element of creating a successful workshop.

Assessing for Writing Workshop

Assessing writers initially is important in shaping your writing curriculum, and ongoing assessment allows you to see not only how students are putting your instruction to use, but also where you need to go with your units, lessons, and conference plans. Teachers choose to handle initial writing assessments in a variety of ways. We'll outline some of the ways that you may choose to use assessment in writing. Whichever way you choose, we want to stress the importance of working from your students' strengths. Rather than looking at a piece of writing and seeing all that might be wrong with the piece—which is the way we were often taught when we were students—we see what students are doing well, and then think about what our immediate and long-term goals are for that particular student, and our class as a whole. We also look at work with an eye toward standards or goals we have in mind. (We have Standards books that serve as guides in New York.) We do this in order to avoid comparing students, and to see where students are, and where they need to be when they leave our classrooms.

Informal Assessments: Surveys, the Writing Notebook, Quick Publish

There are many ways to get a sense of who our students are as writers. First, the writing survey gives you a glimpse into their writing lives. As you read the responses, think about not only what your students are saying, but also how they're saying it. Additionally, the writing notebook provides huge insight into students as writers. Because the notebook is a tool for larger pieces of writing, we are very careful when assessing it. Typically we look to see if the writing is complete and thoughtfully done rather than if the spelling or grammar is correct. We do, however, use what we notice in spelling, grammar, style, and so on, to inform our teaching and our conferring with students. We do not mark up their writer's notebooks with corrections—writer's notebooks are a tool for students.

Writing workshop teachers may also choose to begin the year with a "quick publish" where students take three days to go through the writing cycle. This kind of writing allows you to see not only what your students know about writing mechanics, but also about genre, craft, and the writing process. Obviously if your students are unfamiliar with the writing process it wouldn't make sense to begin this way because you need to teach them about the steps in the process.

Formal Assessments: Rubrics

Formal assessments are done using rubrics. There are a couple of basic ideas about rubrics we want to clarify here. The purpose of using rubrics is both to make clear your expectations as a teacher and to demystify the grading process as a whole. When we use rubrics, we are only evaluating what we've taught our students. That is, we would never mark our students down for not using paragraphs unless we had taught them how and why to use paragraphs. Some teachers might say that at a certain point kids should just be expected to know certain things about writing. The fact of the matter is that they often don't, and marking them down essentially penalizes them for *teachers* they may have had in the past. So, our rubrics always reflect our own teaching. It is important to note that we build on what we've taught, so in our first unit of study, if we've taught paragraphs, then we expect to see students using paragraphs not only in their next publication, but in their writing notebooks and in all of their writing where using paragraphs makes sense.

Our rubrics tend to be in kid-friendly language so that students can clearly understand how and why they got the grade they did. Giving students the rubric ahead of time and allowing them to sit their work alongside the rubric and see where they think they need work lets them take responsibility for their writing. They can clearly see that grading is not based on whim or some unattainable notion inside their teacher's head. It's based on what was taught.

While there is no set way to draw up a rubric, there are set ideas about what one should consist of. The criteria should only be based upon what it is you have taught in the unit or have covered previously in the year. How you come up with a number grade is based upon the practices of your school, district, or region. Some teachers use the traditional scale of 1–100, with each criterion weighing a certain number of points.

However, there is a nationwide movement to grade on a 4-point scale. In compliance with the National Standards, a 4 would mean a student is working above the national standard, a 3 would mean the student is working at the standard, a 2 would mean a student is approaching the standard level, and a 1 would signify the student working below the national standard. (See appendix for sample rubric on 4-point scale.) The teacher would grade each criteria from 1 to 4 and then add up the total number of points. Then, the teacher would divide the total number of points by the total number of criteria on the rubric and get a number divisible by four. That will be the student's score. Example:

Criteria	Above/4	Meets/3	Approaching/2	Below/1
Criteria 1		x		
Criteria 2			x	
Criteria 3		x		
Criteria 4		x		

The above rubric shows that the student got a 3 for criteria 1, a 2 for criteria 2, and a 3 for criterias 3 and 4. So, you would add 3 + 2 + 3 + 3 = 11. Then you'd divide 11 by 4 (because there are four criterias). The student's score would be a 2.7.

When we're thinking about assessment early on in writing workshop, we're really thinking of researching our students. We start with a clear picture of our goals (as teachers, as a grade, as a school district, etc.), nd determine what we need to teach students to reach these goals. Finally, we prioritize our goals and plan our units of study. It is our hope that the writing lessons we're outlining for you will allow you to gather more ideas about your students as writers to serve as a springboard for your planning.

The Workshop Format

Workshop follows a very predictable structure in both reading and writing. Students need structure, especially in middle school. Knowing what to expect helps them to be prepared, to act responsibly, to stay focused, and to be aware of their boundaries within that structure. Teachers often assume that workshop classrooms are free-form because students have choices about their independent work. This couldn't be farther from the truth. In fact, students are supported in their choices by a repeated and familiar structure. Without it, workshop classrooms would be chaotic. The more that teachers maintain a structure to the day, the easier it is to manage the classroom. With that in mind, we want to point out a few of the basic elements of a workshop classroom.

The Mini-Lesson

Each workshop (reading or writing) starts with a mini-lesson. It could be a lesson on behavior or on revising the lead of a story. Whatever the topic, a mini-lesson is short—typically 10 to 20 minutes—and usually entails some modeling of a particular skill or strategy by the teacher. The reason mini-lessons are kept short is because the bulk of a student's learning takes place when he or she is given time to practice that particular skill or strategy. This is the time when the learning is internalized—when the student makes it his or her own.

For mini-lessons to remain mini, teachers need to be very clear in their goals and focused in their instruction. Mini-lessons aren't the time for complex, multistep directions. You want your students to come away with one thing to try. And, like the workshop itself, there's a structure for doing this:

Introduce the Lesson: The teacher introduces the mini-lesson by connecting the current work to students' past work. Creating this connection for students activates their prior knowledge and makes explicit the purpose of their learning that day. You'll notice in the lessons that follow that our introductions are typically short and, through discussion or by means of a chart, always refer to something we've worked on previously.
Teach the Lesson: Here is the bulk of the mini-lesson. The teacher models what the students are to accomplish in reading or writing that day, reading aloud or writing in front of the class. This is also when the teacher explains any charts she has made or when she and the class develop charts together based on her modeling.

The mini-lesson is your chance to tell your students something about the reading or writing process or to teach them a specific skill or strategy to apply to their reading or writing. You will want to make sure you are as clear in your instruction as possible. Use language that your students will understand and model the skills in a way that your students can easily emulate. In preparation for teaching the mini-lesson, we:

- practice our read-alouds ahead of time, marking the connections we want to model with sticky notes;
- create writing examples in advance;
- and visualize or even script the lesson to make sure we will be clear, focused, and brief.

Transition to Independent Work: After modeling the reading or writing strategy or skill in the mini-lesson, the teacher explains how the students themselves will practice it. He may encourage students to share their plan for reading or writing, either with the class or a partner. He may ask students to give the strategy a quick try in the meeting area itself. The teacher must also tell the class how much time they have for independent work, so that they can continue to learn how to budget their time.

The idea behind the Transition is to make sure that students are clear about what it is they are going to do with their independent time before they go off to work. Helping them develop a plan before they work—based on what you've taught during the mini-lesson (or in past mini-lessons)—makes it easier for them to get started once they leave the meeting area. It is an important part of managing the workshop and supporting students in their growing independence.

Independent Work

Students now begin to internalize your teaching by practicing the topic of the mini-lesson on their own. Independent work time is set up to provide students with choices. How they incorporate your teaching into their reading and writing lives, what task they apply it to, and even where they sit are all choices that impact students' sense of self as a readers and writers, and making these decisions will help them develop into lifelong learners.

Students need ample time to read and to write, as the only way they improve at reading and writing is by doing it! And while they practice the lesson, it is our job to confer with them one-on-one—to talk to them about what it is they are doing and how it is affecting their learning.

Conferring

One of the most important elements of the workshop—in fact, the foundation on which students and teachers build their year's study of good reading and writing practices—is the conference, the one-on-one talk between teacher and student about reading and writing, which usually occurs during independent work time. Much has been written about conferring in reading and writing workshop, and, as teachers, we find such texts very helpful. Carl Anderson's *How's It Going?* is invaluable for understanding the structure of conferences; it also gives clear examples of what strong, succinct conferring sounds like. Lucy Calkins' *The Art of Teaching Reading* has a very clear section on conferring with examples of things you might say to students if you notice them doing something specific in their reading work. She also discusses other ways of conferring with students that we found opened up how we looked at conferring with students in our classrooms. We won't reiterate what has been written on the topic, but we do encourage you to seek out these materials. And, as a way of underlining the importance of conferring, we do want to acknowledge that for a first-year teacher, or one new to workshop, it is quite a tricky business.

The following activities comprise the framework of any conference.

- Research the student to discover strengths and needs.
- Make a decision about what you are going to tell him to help him become a better reader or writer.
- Teach him that skill or strategy.
- Note your findings and plan for his progress on a conference sheet.

In our early days of holding reading and writing conferences, we found that we could ask kids generally what was going on in their reading or writing, but were at a loss when it came down to actually teaching something. As a result, many of those initial conferences sounded a lot like this:

Teacher: So, what are you working on in reading today?
Student: I'm on page 10.
Teacher: Okay, what's going on in your book?
Student: Well, I'm making some personal connections.
Teacher: Can you show me one?
Student: Here, I said that Stanley reminds me of my friend because he gets in trouble by accident.
Teacher: Any other personal connections?
Student: Yeah, here I said that this reminds me of the time I went to camp and I was scared to leave my parents but then I had a good time.
Teacher: Okay…so you're doing a good job making personal connections…
Silence
Teacher: Okay, great. So keep going with those!

As our understandings of both conferring and our students as readers and writers grew, our conferences had more purpose to them and became more focused. The more we talk with our students, watch them as they read and write, and listen to what they tell us about themselves and their work as readers and writers, the more we are able to actually teach something during conferences. Essentially, our conferences have became very brief individualized mini-lessons. For instance, sometimes we go in to a conference with a theory in mind about a reader or writer:

Teacher: I wanted to talk with you because I noticed that you were using sticky notes for retelling at the end of every chapter. Can you talk with me a bit about why you do this? [Teacher might be wondering: is this a habit taught in another grade, or does this child do this to carry their understanding of one chapter to the next? If the latter is true, how are those post-it notes helping? Does the child look back on them? If the former is true, how is this helping the student in reading now? How can I change this habit to support the student in becoming a stronger, smarter reader now and in the future?]
Student: Yeah. I do a retell at the end of each chapter.
Teacher: Right. Can you talk to me about why you're doing this? How do you find it helps you as a reader?
Student: Well, it helps me remember the story.
Teacher: Show me one of your sticky notes and talk to me about how you use it to help you remember.
Student: See? Here's one. Okay, so I just write down what happens at the end of the chapter. Then, if I start a new chapter and I'm confused about something, I can go back and reread this note, or other notes to see if things make more sense that way.
Teacher: So, let me make sure I understand you. You're using your retellings to help you hang on to the important parts of the story?

STUDENT: Yeah.

TEACHER: Do you think you have to do that for every chapter at this point?

STUDENT: [Shrugs.]

TEACHER: You might want to think about using retellings more carefully now. As a class we're going to start moving toward looking at characters in our books and developing theories about them. So, we're going to start using sticky notes to mark our thinking in some different ways. Before we do that, you might want to think about these retellings. Maybe you don't need them for every chapter, or maybe you don't need to go into such detail. Some of them are really long, I notice! Maybe you can just edit them down to the important points. [Teacher models this using a read aloud or student's text.] Can you try that?

STUDENT: [Nods.]

TEACHER: Okay, tell me what you're going to do.

STUDENT: Make my retellings more short and only with the important stuff and then see how that goes and make sure it still helps me keep track of the story.

TEACHER: Great. I'll check back with you in a few days to see how it's going.

Other times we found that we had to almost re-teach our mini-lessons to students in conferences. The only time we worried about doing that was when we noticed we had to do it with many students. That let us know that something must have been unclear in our whole-class teaching and that we should revisit it as a class. Our conferences don't always sound like the ones outlined in this text. Often we support something that a student is already doing, guide them through a rough patch, or just talk about something they're doing as a reader or writer. But, for the beginning workshop teacher, understanding that you need to learn something about what your students are doing and teach them something to support their reading and writing lives, is a huge step. Gaining confidence in conferring and using it to plan your curriculum is one of the most powerful things you can learn as a teacher.

Classroom Management During Conference

Students need to understand that they should be ready to talk about their reading and writing at all times—not necessarily what their reading or writing is about, but what they're doing as readers and writers. They need to know how to talk about the choices they're making, the things they are thinking about, the purposes behind their work, and what they're learning. They should also know that when you are conferring with another student, they are to be reading or writing independently. They should not talk, nor should they interrupt your conference for anything other than a true emergency.

Know that the purpose of a conference is to teach a student something about reading or writing. Conferences are short—only about 5 to 10 minutes—so that you can see as many students as possible in one period. You need to record what you've done in a conference in order to keep track of a child's learning. (See an example of one of our conference records, right.) A good idea is to prepare children for conferences with a mini-lesson about some of the questions you'll ask, what your notes are for, and why you confer. Often, these kinds of mini-lessons help give children the language they need to begin talking about themselves in a more reflective way.

Make your expectations clear to the entire class—there's no way you can confer with one student if the rest of the room is loud and chaotic. We know all too well that keeping a class of 30 or more middle-school students on track while you confer with one can be rough in the beginning. Your initial conferences may be mere check-ins as you keep the rest of your class on task. We've found that teaching management mini-lessons about what independent work time looks like and sounds like is helpful in this regard, as is establishing clear rules backed up by sensible consequences.

We don't expect that you'll be conferring with ease by the end of these 30 lessons. But we hope that the lessons will help you gain that ease over time. We've provided tips for how to respond to common issues, as well as examples of what conferring sounds like. The more you practice conferring, the better you'll get. Your students will become accustomed to it and grow more independent in their learning and work. Establishing conference routines now will make it easier for you to continue workshop and will make it possible for you to try more sophisticated teaching down the line, such as guided reading groups and book clubs.

CONFERENCE SHEET

DATE:
SUBJECT:

RESEARCH — DECIDE — TEACH

CONFERRED WITH: Edwin	DISCUSSED: (How Can I Help? What's my Theory?)	POSSIBLE MINI-LESSONS: (Strategies/Suggestions to address Student's Questions/Concerns)
7/10	taking a break Drown Help I'm a Prisoner in the Library! Thinki	
7/12	word attack skills Bridges	Thinking of using pictures for words he doesn't know.
7/16		need to make a commitment to a book
7/17	chose Dear Mr. Henshaw retelling: wrote a letter? hasn't got to him yet · maybe he'll call?	teaching inferrences need to [illegible] EVIDENCE Making sure reading MAKES SENSE
7/18	must [illegible] pin are for retelling personal connection	Reading CLOSELY being able to retell:
7/24	text-to-text responses: both about basketball, same topic 2 genres.	*looking for things when we read.

COMMENTS/OBSERVATIONS/PLANS FOR WHOLE CLASS INSTRUCTION:

7/25	Reading making sense: be strong if you want to play basketball theme	how to make connections about differences in books.
7/27	Doesn't get "style"	writing style—knowing how to see this stuff. (thinking about connections)

A sample conference sheet for a fifth grader.

Reflect on the Day's Work/Share Our Ideas

After students have practiced the lesson and you've had a chance to confer with individuals, it is very important that they share their thoughts about it as a class. It is crucial for them as learners to feel that their perspectives and ideas are valued and appreciated, not only by you but also by their classmates. We've found that many teachers who are just beginning workshop and coping with time constraints will often drop this part. We urge you not to.

If you've ever spent time with middle-school students, you'll surely agree that they listen to each other much more than they ever listen to their teacher! This is the time to capitalize on that. Providing the time for students to share their ideas allows them to feel successful; it teaches them to listen and to value each other as learners. It is also a way of making sure that they understand the day's work, a last opportunity for clearing up misunderstandings or just reinforcing the ideas of the lesson. Sometimes a student won't have understood your explanation during the modeling or a conference, but hearing a peer explain what they did can make all the difference. This is really a time for kids to teach one another.

As middle-school teachers, we've noticed that there is very little time in the day for students to talk with one another. They shuttle from class to class, stealing moments in the hallways, bathrooms, or when your back is turned to engage in important conversations. (They may not seem important to you, but to a twelve-year-old, the discovery that a girl in class 704 is wearing the exact same outfit can be a matter or life or death!) And students rarely have time to speak about intellectual matters. As teachers, we're so concerned that they hear us that we avoid allowing them to talk to one another for fear that we'll lose control.

It is, however, important that we set up rules of conduct and a structure for the time when students share their ideas. We do have to insure that feelings aren't hurt and everyone has a voice in their classroom.

We've learned wonderful things from our students during share time. We encourage you to make the time to do the same.

Classroom Environment

Teaching Reading and Writing Workshop requires a special classroom environment, one that supports not only reading and writing but also independence and the workshop process. What this environment looks like depends on the vision of a particular school or teacher, but certain basic things should be in place:

- a classroom library;
- places where students and teacher can meet in large and small groups;
- and places where individuals can work quietly.

A room that is well organized is often as important to your teaching as your lesson plans are, especially in those first few weeks of school. To your students the classroom setup communicates your sense of order, your expectations about how they will conduct themselves, and what they will be asked to do. The placement of your desk—or whether you even have a desk—sends a message about how you will conduct yourself. When setting up our classrooms, we've kept in mind our main goal as literacy teachers: to have our students reading and writing as much as possible throughout the year. We've tried to make those areas that support reading and writing the central focus of our classrooms, so that as soon as students, parents, or other teachers enter the room, our goals are evident.

Moreover, a neat, warm, colorful, and inviting classroom can do wonders for the sense of community. It sends the clear message to your students that you care enough about your experience together—that you care enough about them—to make your surroundings beautiful.

The Classroom Library

A classroom library is the heart and soul of the literacy classroom. You can communicate this by positioning the library prominently in the classroom. Some teachers choose to put bookshelves all over the room, which allows many children to view books at once. Others, including us, choose to have a section of the room devoted to the classroom library. We made cozy reading areas with rugs and pillows where kids could snuggle up with their books. We've found this is especially nice for independent reading, but we do have to teach students how to behave in this area, setting rules of conduct, like how many pillows each person is allowed to have, whether it's okay to save seats, and so on.

Stocking the Library

The classroom library should contain a wide variety of books, spanning different genres and reading levels. We recommend arranging books in bins or baskets with the covers visible, since this makes it more likely that students, and especially reluctant readers, will spend time looking at books. Kids are more inclined to look at a book, open it up, and read one or two pages if they can see the cover than if all they can see is the book's spine among other spines lined up on a shelf.

Most important, your library needs to contain books that reflect the interests and the various reading levels of your students. The best classroom libraries support students reading on, below, and above grade level. For example, in a 6th-grade classroom, a teacher may want to have books that range from 2nd- to 8th-grade reading levels. Since the majority of our students tend to read below grade level, we provide them with a range of high-interest, low-level reading books. In our first years of teaching, we thought those books were difficult to find, but now we notice that there are more and more offerings, in bookstores and online.

Nonfiction texts should not be overlooked. We've found that it is easier to find lower-level nonfiction texts—on shark attacks, aliens, and famous baseball players, for example—that will interest struggling middle-school readers.

Organizing the Library

How teachers organize their baskets or bins depends on their curriculum, the size of their library, and what they choose to communicate or teach about reading. Most teachers organize by genre, including bins for poetry, fantasy and science fiction, autobiography, and so on. You can also create categories of books that support connections with student writing, such as baskets for mentor or touchstone texts (texts with which students are familiar that are serving as models for their writing), and read-alouds. We've used baskets for individual authors, award-winners, class favorites, and monthly recommendations.

Many people suggest separating lower-level books from the rest of the library, so that struggling readers can find them more easily. We've found that struggling readers avoid lower-level book baskets like the plague! Instead, we mix lower-level books into our libraries. We also hold conferences with students about choosing books that are right for them, talk-up the shorter texts in our classrooms, and have honest conversations with our classes about how reading books that feel comfortable—even easy—is the way to become stronger readers. As a result, an increased number of lower-level readers find texts that are right for them, and they're not ashamed of their choices.

To support good book choices early in the year, we recommend that teachers limit their lending library to shorter texts, even lower-level books. Many students don't know what it feels like to read a book that is on their level. Others might be embarrassed to choose books that are shorter, wanting to present themselves as "good" readers who read "big" books. Limiting the library increases the chances of students picking "just-right" books. After you have assessed your class, figured out the approximate levels of all your students, and discussed book choice, then you can begin to introduce longer and more challenging books.

Keeping Track of Books

It is important to have a well-organized system of circulation—the taking out and returning of books. This system should be simple enough for students to navigate on their own without causing a major disturbance to you or to their classmates. We've seen teachers who tape pockets in the back of books and have their students use a date stamp like real librarians. Others simply have a sign-out book, with monitors making sure that students return their books on time. Most middle-school students would lose their heads if they weren't attached, so it is important to do everything you can to make sure your books are returned!

Ultimately, students need to have access to good, engaging books. The more they read, with support and independently, the better they become at reading and writing. Having a full and diverse classroom library encourages students to make reading part of their lives.

The Meeting Area

In most workshop classrooms, the mini-lesson and share time take place in a meeting area—a place where students and teacher can come together, where they can see and hear one another. Because mini-lessons are just that—mini—teachers need to make sure that students are listening.

Some teachers choose to have their meeting area on a rug in the corner of the room, around an easel or an overhead projector, so that they can display charts. Other teachers choose an area in the middle of the room and surround it with tables for independent work. Whatever you decide, meeting in that area should become routine for your class, part of a ritual. Students should know to go there with their reading or writing notebooks at the start of the lesson.

Some teachers are concerned that they do not have enough space to create a meeting area. But we've seen successful workshops—led by strong teachers—during which students simply pulled their chairs in closer or turned their bodies to see the board for a mini-lesson. While such solutions may work, we feel that they're not ideal, since they don't promote the sense of community that is created when students come together. In fact, squeezing students together into a small meeting area can be an extremely helpful management tool, since you don't have to pace around the room to maintain order. Using a small space also can really help new teachers, who often find it challenging to negotiate the transitions to and from the meeting area.

We've always had great success with our meeting areas, whether in small classrooms stuffed with big 8th graders or large rooms with comparatively tiny 5th graders. We encourage you to create a meeting area in your classroom.

Independent Work Areas

In a typical workshop classroom, students have different spaces in which to work. A student can read a book curled up on a rug or sit around a table participating in a book talk. Writing can happen at tables or on the floor in the meeting area, notebook propped on knees. If students can handle choosing their own places to work, they should do so. If you're choosing between tables and desks, we recommend tables, since they can be moved and used with small or large groups.

Some teachers also choose to have areas in the room that support the workshop; often they're called reading, writing, or publishing centers. There you might stock draft paper, pens and pencils, bookmarks, sticky notes, staplers, rulers, tape, and so on. A monitor could volunteer or be chosen to make sure that students return pens or pencils and care for the supplies. Teachers may choose to keep In and Out boxes in these centers for collecting notebooks or drafts and for returning them.

However your room is organized, it should support students' independence. This will be helpful when you're holding conferences because if your students can work independently, they won't constantly interrupt you.

Charts become valuable references in workshop classrooms, helping students become independent learners.

Charts

You might notice that workshop teachers make many charts! When we launched Reading and Writing Workshop in our school, our colleagues often referred to us as the "charters." They teased us about the number of charts we brought in because, as teachers in traditional classrooms, they just didn't understand the methods of the workshop.

The workshop teacher creates charts so that students spend less time mindlessly copying. Hanging charts in your classroom creates a print-rich environment that supports student independence. The walls of your classroom become a reference book for your kids. Therefore, how you organize your charts is important—if you want your students to refer to the charts you hang in your classroom, they'll need to understand the arrangement. We usually divide our rooms into Reading Workshop and Writing Workshop and label the areas. We post most of the reading charts in the areas around our classroom library, so that students can read charts on finding "just-right" books, the library rules, or ways a reader might respond to a book. Our writing charts are often hung around our writing centers, so that as students gather drafting paper, they can see a model drafting plan. The wall space around the meeting area can be used for posting charts that reflect our work for that day. Organizing our charts and referring to them in our lessons makes it easier for students working independently to find answers on their own, which means

also that conferences are seldom interrupted. While the use of charts is integral to the workshop classroom, it is important that you not wallpaper your room with outdated or irrelevant material. That is, charts should be student-centered, student-generated, and relevant to the current unit of study.

In a workshop classroom, the more organized you can be, the more smoothly your days will run. It is vital to arrange your classroom in ways that support your educational objectives as well as your students' efforts, growth, and independence, especially when launching Reading and Writing Workshop.

Getting Started With Reading Writing Workshop

This section has provided an overview of the Reading and Writing Workshop. Once you've arranged the classroom, determined your schedule, and greeted your students, you are ready to begin. The 30 lessons that follow will help you establish the routines and teach the processes you'll need for a year of successful reading and writing. The very first lesson, which begins on the next page, introduces the idea of a workshop, explains the materials students will need, and establishes expectations for behavior. The structure of workshop is the same for reading and writing—mini-lesson, independent work, conferring, share—so the ideas in this lesson apply to both kinds of workshops.

After teaching this first lesson, outline your schedule for Reading and Writing Workshop, reading on Monday, Wednesday, Friday, writing on Tuesday and Thursday, for example. Let students know when you'll begin this schedule (we recommend diving right in the first week of school). Then move through the lessons sequentially, taking your time and responding to the needs of your students. At the conclusion of this unit of study, which usually takes a little more than a month, students will be familiar with the workshop structure, and you'll be well on your way to year's worth of rich literacy teaching. Good luck!

The Lessons

Several overarching goals guided the planning of this unit of study. By the end of it, your students should be able to:

- write independently for at least 30 minutes, staying on task;
- read independently for at least 30 minutes, staying on task;
- understand the workshop structure and how to move quickly through the transitions;
- comfortably share their writing and ideas with their classmates;
- follow their thoughts as they read, understanding that good readers make connections to the text;
- understand each stage of the Writing Cycle, ready to begin a new writing study that will focus less on process and more on craft.

Introducing the Workshop

By the end of this lesson, students will:

- have gotten to know one another as readers and writers;
- understand that there are expectations about their conduct that need to be respected for the class to work well together;
- understand the daily rituals of the workshop.

Preparation:

1. Make a class set of copies of the reading and writing survey (see Appendix, pp. 138–139).
2. Create three charts. These charts have worked for us:

Chart A:
Every Day We Will:
1. Gather at the meeting area for a reading or writing mini-lesson (15–20 minutes);
2. Work independently in a comfortable space (30–45 minutes);
3. Confer with [add your name here];
4. Share our work at the meeting area (10 minutes).

Chart B:
Supplies Needed:
1. 2 thick marble note-books; one for reading, one for writing
2. 2 folders, one for reading, one for writing
3. Pencils, pens, and highlighters
4. A few packages of sticky notes

Chart C
Expectations Chart:
To Make Workshop Work, We Agree to:
1. Be here on time every day;
2. Be prepared to work hard;
3. Always bring our supplies and assignments;
4. Support learning by respecting each other's ideas and work;
5. Read and write every day.

Introduce the Lesson:

Before you begin today's mini-lesson, we suggest that you review charts A, B, and C with your class. Spend time making your expectations clear, letting students know what supplies they will need and what the daily ritual of workshop will look like. Charts A, B, and C are meant to support your main objective for today and your work throughout the year.

In our experience, the first few days set the tone for the rest of the year. We have found that it is important to convey our passion for reading and writing at the beginning of the school year to encourage students to realize their own.

This year we're going to be reading and writing a lot! One of the most important things we will be doing is examining the habits and thoughts of good readers and writers. For this to happen, we need to create an environment where people can work and feel safe taking risks in their reading and writing.

Teach the Lesson:

We need to begin thinking of ourselves as readers and writers. I'd like you to think of the good things we have accomplished and the struggles you have faced. Thoughtful readers and writers take time to reflect on themselves and their own learning.

I am passing out two surveys that we're going to take some time to fill out. Let's go over the questions to make sure they're clear to you.

Read aloud each question on the survey below, making sure students know what is being asked and how to thoughtfully answer the questions.

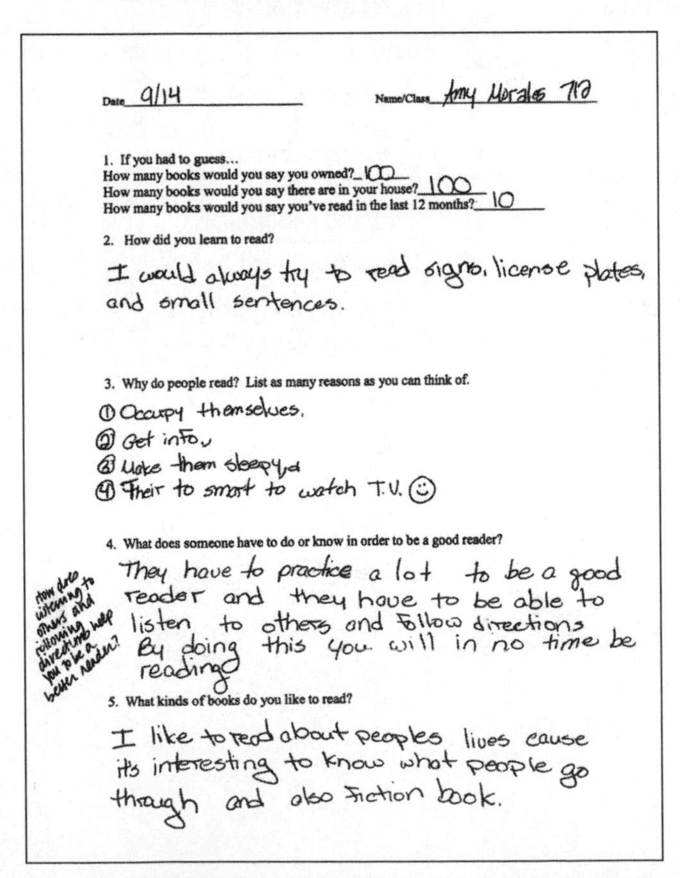

Date 9/14 Name/Class Amy Morales 712

1. If you had to guess...
How many books would you say you owned? 100
How many books would you say there are in your house? 100
How many books would you say you've read in the last 12 months? 10

2. How did you learn to read?
I would always try to read signs, license plates, and small sentences.

3. Why do people read? List as many reasons as you can think of.
① Occupy themselves.
② Get info.
③ Make them sleepy.
④ Their to smart to watch T.V. ☺

4. What does someone have to do or know in order to be a good reader?
They have to practice a lot to be a good reader and they have to be able to listen to others and follow directions By doing this you will in no time be reading
(How does listening to others and following directions help you to be a better reader?)

5. What kinds of books do you like to read?
I like to read about peoples lives cause it's interesting to know what people go through and also fiction book.

6. How do you decide what books to read?
I look at the pictures, title, author, and I read the back summary.
(Great strategies.)

7. Who are your favorite authors? (List as many as possible)
Gary Paulsen
Jane Thayer

8. Have you ever reread a book? Yes If so, can you name it/them here?
Emerald Enjoyed The Moonlight, The True Story of the 3 little Pigs, The Stinky Cheese Man & other Fairly Stupid Tales.

9. What is the title of the last book you read? When did you finish this book?
The Secret of Skull Mountain
8/13/99

10. How often do you read at home?
All the Time

11. In general, how do you feel about reading?
I like the way I read because I'm always getting compliments.
(What do you get compliments about?)

Sample reading survey adapted from Nancie Atwell (1998).

Transition to Independent Work:

You will have about 20 minutes to complete this survey. I will be walking around, observing how you work, and talking with some of you.

This is a good time to refer to Chart A to show students that they are moving through the ritual of workshop.

Be thoughtful in your writing, write as much as you can, and use the full time to write. Take a minute to find a comfortable workspace where you think you can get a lot of writing done.

This is the time to build the foundation of the workshop structure. Getting your rituals in place now will help establish smooth transitions between the mini-lesson and independent work, allowing for deeper learning later. You might consider creating a way to help your students transition between the mini-lesson to independent time, and from independent time to share time. You could count down, ring a bell, or coin a phrase such as, "Let's get started" to signify that students should switch tasks.

Confer with Students:

While students are working independently, watch how they behave. Ask yourself, Who gets started right away? Who has trouble being independent? Who is writing a great deal? Who is struggling to fill the page? Who says, "I'm done!" quickly? Too quickly? Keeping notes on your observations can help you understand the needs of individual students.

Since today is the first class, you will probably spend more time observing your students than talking with them. However, use your discretion. If a student needs individual attention, then have a small conference.

As you walk around, find a few students who are willing to share parts of their survey with the class.

Reflect on the Day's Work/Share Our Ideas:

Signal the transition to share time. Discuss some of your positive observations with your students.

I noticed that many of you were writing a great deal about your reading and writing life. Would a few of you like to share what you wrote?

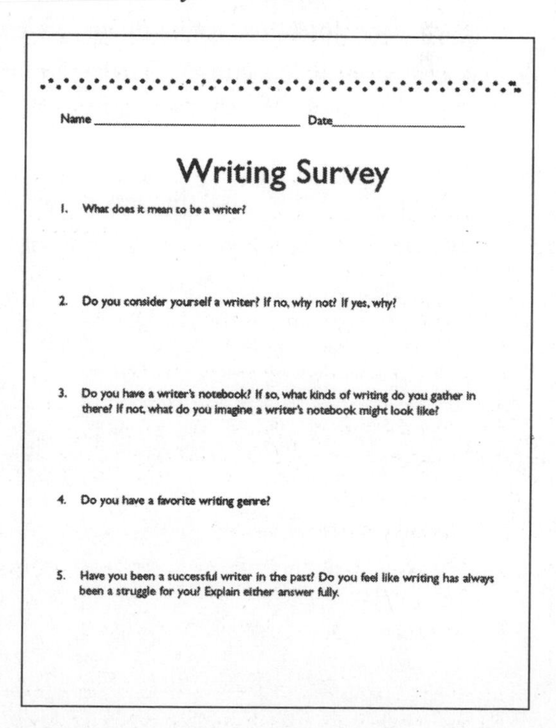

Name ______________ Date ______________

Writing Survey

1. What does it mean to be a writer?

2. Do you consider yourself a writer? If no, why not? If yes, why?

3. Do you have a writer's notebook? If so, what kinds of writing do you gather in there? If not, what do you imagine a writer's notebook might look like?

4. Do you have a favorite writing genre?

5. Have you been a successful writer in the past? Do you feel like writing has always been a struggle for you? Explain either answer fully.

Follow-up:

- *For homework, students should write about the first book they remember reading or the first essay they wrote in school.*
- *To reinforce the importance of their work outside the classroom, review the Expectations Chart with your students before the end of the lesson.*

The Writing Workshop

In the writing workshop, we strive to make students see themselves as writers. Hopefully, the myth of the author as a genius who sits down and pounds out a book is debunked. The idea of talent is played down while the suggestions of process and hard work are reinforced. While the process itself is imposed, students write from their own experiences using their own unique voices.

The workshop is a place to celebrate all kinds of writers. We use the writing process to help students gather and refine their ideas before placing them on a paper to be graded. We aim to teach students a way of life, to build in them a passion for the written word. We strive to create an atmosphere where students feel safe to take risks and get crafty with their writing.

The Teacher's Writing Notebook

During the entire first unit of study, we rely heavily on modeling to convey the different parts of the writing process in the clearest, most visual way. When we introduce the writer's notebook to a new group of students, we usually walk them through an example of a good one. We always share our own notebooks as a way to create a community of trust and respect in the classroom. It helps students get to know us as writers, seeing that we, too, go through the writing process. Also, because we have this resource, we usually show the class a student notebook from the past year.

If you are new to the Writing Workshop, you will need to use your own notebook to launch writing in your class. Therefore, we strongly recommend that you build your notebook before launching the study. It might be a good idea to have at least fifteen entries before you begin. Since the point is to let your kids leaf through your notebook, reading your work, they will know that your notebook is not authentic if it's brand new and has only five entries. Starting a notebook may seem like a daunting proposition, but many teachers we have worked with find it helpful and inspiring. Those teachers who had not been writing regularly found their writing voice once again.

Use the first five collecting lessons we have provided to launch your notebook. From these lessons, you should be able to get a good sense of what a writing notebook looks like and be able to generate many, many more entries.

Collecting Lesson #1: Launching the Writing Notebook

By the end of this lesson, students will:
- know the purpose of a writer's notebook;
- have begun collecting entries in their own notebooks.

Preparation:
1. Create a blank chart titled What [your name] Wrote About in Her and His Writer's Notebook.
2. Review your writing notebook and flag entries you plan to read aloud.

Introduce the Lesson:

Before we even begin our first writing lesson, I wanted to review how the workshop will flow. Even if we are working on reading, workshop structure is the same every day. *Review chart A from yesterday's lesson briefly with the students.* Every day we will meet at the rug for our mini-lesson and then split up to work independently. After we work quietly, we will meet again as a group for the share. Are there any questions about how we will move through the workshop today?

This is only the second lesson! In our experience, it can take days before the students move through the rituals of workshop in a clear and consistent manner. Don't get discouraged if your students are noisy when first moving from the gathering area to the independent areas or if they find it difficult to work independently. However, don't allow the unruly behavior to continue.

Have them practice movement throughout the room if necessary. If need be, for the first few days of class, stand back and watch them while they work independently. These interventions may take up a great deal of time, especially at the beginning of the year. In fact, they should take up your time! After all, this is new to your students. They need to learn the appropriate behaviors at the onset of the school year. Review your expectations and have them practice, practice, practice. The launching of the workshop sets the tone for the rest of your year. We suggest you take the time to set up the classroom structures now so that the rest of the year runs smoothly.

We already know that we'll be reading a great deal in class this year because good readers read a lot! We'll also be writing a great deal in class and at home because good writers write a lot. We will write for 20 minutes today. By the middle of the year, we should be able to write for 40 minutes at a time. Where will we do all this writing? Well, today, I am going to show you where. *Hold up your writer's notebook.*

Teach the Lesson:

This is my writer's notebook. Your notebooks are brand new and very clean looking. My notebook is not. I spent some time decorating my notebook to make it feel more personal. You might want to decorate your notebook at home tonight.

You might choose to spend time showing your students how you personalized your notebook.

My notebook is a few weeks old and already has... *Rifle through notebook, counting the entries...* 20 entries in it! Your notebooks will soon look like this one. I'd like to walk you through my notebook, sharing what it looks like with you. Please pay close attention. I want you to be able to tell me what kinds of entries I have written.

You should take your students through your notebook page by page. Read the titles to them and two or three short entries. Use the following language to help you discuss your notebook:

Let's see. On the first page, you will notice I made a list. That's a list of different ideas I had for my notebook. I wrote down some ideas I had that I wanted to write more about, like when I went hiking with my husband. I want to write about that, so I put it on the list. The next few pages are about my grandmother and some of the memories I have of her when she was alive. This page I folded down because it is a poem I wrote when I was on a hayride last year. On this page I jotted down some favorite quotes by some authors I love. On the next page I wrote about my new son, William. Let me share it with you: *William. William sat up today for the very first time and he stared at me with such a proud expression on his face. I felt as though he would just get up and walk at any moment. William. We gave him a strong name. The name of poets and writers and powerful people. William. He is already very powerful because he has changed my life forever. Continue sharing snippets of your notebook with your students. Stop when you feel they get the idea.*

Take about two minutes and quickly jot down some of the things I wrote about.

Give just two minutes. Everyone will work right at the meeting area. At this time, you should display the blank chart called What [your name] Wrote About in Her or His Writer's Notebook.

What did I write about in my notebook?

Spend a few minutes writing down students' ideas. Your chart may look something like the one below.

WHAT [your name] WROTE ABOUT IN HER OR HIS WRITER'S NOTEBOOK

She wrote about personal thoughts.

She wrote about her memories.

She shared her wishes and dreams.

She wrote a favorite poem. She wrote about trees.

She collected leaves and taped them in the book.

She wrote about a movie she saw.

She wrote one sentence about her father five times.

She wrote down a favorite quotation.

She voiced her opinions.

She kept a list of writing ideas.

She wrote about everything that happens on her block.

Transition to Independent Work:

I am really glad I shared my notebook with you. Sometimes that can be scary—sharing the insides of your mind with everyone. But you were so respectful of my thoughts and ideas that you made me feel safe. So thanks! I hope you will feel safe with me today when you begin writing in your notebooks.

Let's review this chart we wrote again. *Read it out loud.* I know that many of you are ready to get started, but let's take a few minutes to think about what you will write about today. Feel free to borrow any ideas from my notebook. Writers borrow ideas from each other all the time.

Ask two or three students to share what they will write about today.

I expect that you will write for 20 minutes today. Keep writing until I tell you it is time to stop. If you are ready to begin, go and find a comfortable space for yourself, where you will be able to get your work done. If you are not ready to work alone, stay here and we will look through my notebook again for ideas.

Signal the transition to independent work.

Confer with Students:

Not everyone will be ready and eager to go off and write independently, but we anticipate that most kids will want to try. However, every class is unique. You may have one, two, or ten kids that do not have a good sense of the notebook. Hold a brief conference with them. Let them flip through your notebook again.

You will find it helpful to identify a few students who are willing to volunteer during share time. This will ensure that your share time runs smoothly.

Reflect on the Day's Work/Share Our Ideas:

Signal the end of independent work and the beginning of share time. Students should be at the meeting area within one minute.

I am very proud of you today. I saw many of you settle in very quickly. You were respectful of the writers around you and were very serious about your own work. I also noticed that some students who were stuck for an idea met with me for a group conference. That is also a quality of a good writer—someone who asks for help and does not give up easily.

Ask questions that will allow for deep thinking. You want your students to make connections between what was taught and what was accomplished during independent work time.

Was it helpful to look at my notebook as a way to get started today? Did anyone use an idea from my notebook as a way to write? Could you share your entry or part of your entry with the class?

Have a student that used an idea from your notebook share his entry.

Would anyone else like to share what he or she worked on today?

It's important to foster the sense that sharing is safe. Let them know that they can share a group of words they wrote, just the topic of their work, or even their thoughts about getting started.

Follow-up:

- *For homework, students should write a new entry in their notebooks.*
- *You may find some students writing very short entries. To help them, you may want to use your notebook as a model for longer entries.*

Collecting Lesson #2: Creating a Life Map

By the end of this lesson, students will:
- understand where they are in the writing process;
- have created personal Life Maps and used them as inspiration for independent writing.

Preparation:
1. Make a bright, colorful illustration of the Writing Cycle to hang in the classroom (see below).
2. Draw your personal Life Map on chart paper.
3. In your notebook, write about a symbol from your Life Map, and post the entry on a chart or copy it to handouts.
4. Collect a few copies of *My Grandmother's Hair* by Cynthia Rylant for conferences.

Introduce the Lesson:

The last time we met, we looked at my writer's notebook and discussed the kinds of things I wrote. Let's go over that chart again.

Briefly, review the chart called What [your name] Wrote About in Her or His Writer's Notebook.

Since our last writing workshop, you should have written at least one new entry in your writer's notebooks.

I have two purposes for today's mini-lesson. First, I'd like to talk to you about the bigger picture and why I have asked you to collect these entries. And second, I am going to share another method for collecting entries in your writer's notebooks.

Teach the Lesson:

First, let's discuss the bigger picture. Good writers use a special process to help them write We will be learning all about the writing process throughout the year and will be using it to better ourselves as authors.

Display your colorful posters. You could ask different students to help hold up each one.

There are eight steps that we go through in the Writing Cycle. As our study progresses, we will learn a lot about each of these stages, and I will define each one for you. The different stages are called Collecting (this is where we are now), Reflecting, Choosing, Nurturing, Drafting, Revising, Editing, and Publishing. During the first stage, Collecting, writers do just that: They collect many, many ideas by writing a lot, and collecting as many different kinds of entries in our notebooks as we can is our short-term goal. Our long-term goal is to publish a final work in about four weeks. How we get there is by following the Writing Cycle.

It is important that you are aware that there is a process we use to create written projects. You will be graded on the whole process, not just on one final project. This will include your writing notebook, all the assignments I give you, and your class work and participation.

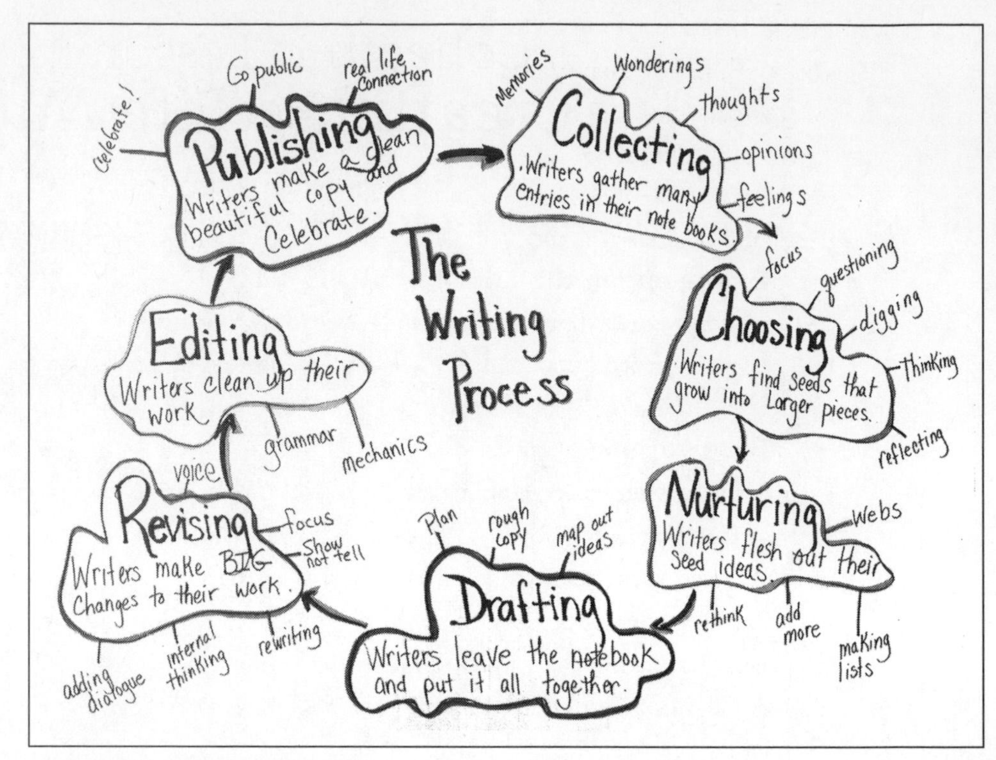

A sample writing process chart.

I wanted you to have a bigger sense of what we are doing here. However, today, we are still collecting entries in our notebooks—the first step in the Writing Cycle.

Point to Collecting on the Writing Cycle chart.

Now that we've discussed the Writing Cycle and where we are in it, I'd like to share another collecting technique to give you more writing ideas.

The Life Map is a really great way for your students to connect with you as a human being. This is your opportunity to reveal a funny childhood antic or momentous occasion in your life. It will help them identify with you.

Display your Life Map. (Be sure to prepare the Life Map ahead of time. The sample Life Map (see page 31) can give you an idea of what yours might look like. You should make it on a large piece of chart paper, so that all your students can see it.)

Choose one symbol from your Life Map to write about. Use an overhead projector, handouts, or chart paper, so that each child has access to your work.

This is my Life Map. It helps me reflect on my memories and think about the stories I have to tell. You will notice I have drawn pictures for different events that have happened in my life. Let me share my map with you.

Use the following language to guide the discussion of your Life Map.

The first symbol on my map is a cup of hot chocolate. I drew this picture because I love hot chocolate and because it makes me think of snow. I love snow and I have many memories of snow. The next symbol on my map is of a diamond ring. This represents the day my husband asked me to marry him. I have many memories about that day and I could write a great deal about them. Another symbol on my map is of a book. I chose this symbol because I loved reading as a child. I thought I could write about my favorite book, *Nana Upstairs and Nana Downstairs* by Tomic Dc Paola.

Continue by discussing the other symbols on your map.

I made this map to help me get more ideas for my notebook. Let me show you how I wrote an entry based on my Life Map.

The following excerpt is provided to give you an idea of what writing based on the map looks like:

A sample life map, a helpful tool for generating writing ideas.

> Life Map Entry # 1
> I remember running to the children's section of the public library. I would run all the way to the back room and all the way to the back shelves. My fingers would scan the bookbindings, searching for the tan one that read *Nana Upstairs and Nana Downstairs* by Tomie De Paola. I loved that book about a grandmother and great-grandmother. It touched my heart every time it was read to me. It still does. Even at twenty-seven, I still cry when the grandmother dies.

Share your entry with the class. It should be at least two pages, so that students will strive to write as much.

Transition to Independent Work:

During independent work time, allow your students to talk with one another while drawing their Life Maps. You may want to use this as an opportunity for reviewing workshop rules or how to work together and stay on task. Whatever route you choose, we highly recommend that discussion take place during this exercise. Students become inspired to write as their classmates' tales are spun and their own memories are relived.

Hand out blank paper and crayons.

I would like you to draw your Life Map. Make sure when you are finished that you staple your map into your writing notebook. While you draw, feel free to discuss your stories and ideas with a partner. Would someone like to share something they plan to draw on the map?

Allow two or three students to share their ideas.

After you are finished drawing the map, you should begin writing about one of the symbols. You should spend about 20 minutes creating the map and then begin writing. I will walk around to make sure you are on task and getting the job done.

During independent work today, we suggest that you remind students when 20 minutes has passed, so that they'll begin writing on time.

Signal the transition to independent work.

Confer with Students:

You will probably encounter a few students who are having trouble creating the Life Map. They will tell you that they haven't been around long enough to have had many big things happen to them. You could share My Grandmother's Hair *by Cynthia Rylant with those students. Rylant takes a very tiny memory about a girl brushing her grandmother's hair and blows it up. The memoir is beautifully written and is a good example of how an author can expand what seems to be a single moment. The conference should teach students that not every memory on the Life Map needs to be a huge event, like the birth of a brother or graduating from fifth grade. Sipping hot cocoa on a rainy day with Daddy is also a memory for the Life Map and would make for very good writing. If you cannot find the Rylant text, feel free to use another memoir.*

It is very easy to overlook your "fast" writers. After all, they don't seem to need your help. Often, students who write about ten pages in 40 minutes merely spill out events. They give the play-by-play and fail to see the deeper significance in their topic. Ask these students questions about their work that will stimulate reflection and deeper thinking. Ask questions that may get a student to open up to you: What is your writing about? Why did you choose to write about this? You have a lot of ideas. Why did you choose this one?

As students talk, they may reveal a significance behind their writing that at first they didn't realize. Help them add this to their notebook.

Reflect on the Day's Work/Share Our Ideas:

Signal the transition to share time. Ask volunteers to share their Life Maps by briefly explaining a few of the symbols. Have other students share their entries, explaining the connections to the symbols on the maps.

Follow-up:

- *For homework, students should complete one more entry from the Life Map.*
- *If you haven't already, you should begin thinking about how to hold the students accountable for their work. Do they know when you will collect the notebooks? Are the notebooks going to be graded? If so, how? Do you have your own notebook rubric? (See Appendix for the Notebook Rubric.) Keeping up with the notebooks can become very time consuming. Consider a rotating schedule, collecting about five notebooks each day.*

Collecting Lesson #3: Ideas for the Writing Notebook

By the end of this lesson, students will:

- have shared the entries they have written in their notebooks;
- have generated a class reference chart of writing ideas;
- understand how they will be graded on the writing they collect in their notebooks.

Preparation:

1. Supply blank chart paper.
2. Supply copies of the Notebook Rubric (see Appendix, p. 140).

Introduce the Lesson:

I am so proud of the work you have been accomplishing in your notebooks. You are doing such a great job of collecting.

It is helpful to refer to the Writing Cycle chart whenever you discuss where students are in the process.

While many of you have been writing a lot, I know that there are times when you feel stuck for an idea. Today, I want to show you another way to get ideas for your notebook.

Teach the Lesson:

It is very common for good writers to get ideas for their notebooks from other writers. Take a few minutes and review your entries. I would like you to be able to share some writing ideas with the class. Turn and talk to someone next to you about some of the things you have written about so far.

Listen to your students' conversations while they discuss their writing.

As I walked around, I heard many wonderful writing ideas. I'd like to fill out a great big chart of all of those ideas. This way, when you are stuck for an idea, you will be able to refer to this great big list. Would anyone like to begin?

Basically, you want to hold a brainstorming session. The most efficient way to do this is to have students talk out their ideas as you chart them.

You may choose to title the chart Ideas for Our Writer's Notebooks. *You may have to reduce students' subjects to one- or two-word categories. Your chart should end up looking something like this:*

Memories
Dreams
Wishes
Movies you liked
Favorite sports
Embarrassing moments
Family
Trips and vacations
School
The future
World events
Opinions
Questions
Love
Anger
Favorite place
Heroes
Singers
Break-ups
Valentine's Day
Holidays
Pets
Winter
Summer
The park
The beach
Great Adventure
Best friends
Recipes
Poetry
Deep thoughts
Food
Culture

You have four minutes to copy this list in the back of your writing notebooks.

Transition to Independent Work:

You should be finished copying the list. I'd like you to choose two new ideas that you will write about today. You can write about anything on the list, or you can come up with a new idea. Turn and talk to the person next to you about what you will write about today. When you are ready to begin writing, you may leave the meeting area and work independently. We will write for 40 minutes today, and I will walk around around to confer with you while you work.

You may consider writing in your notebook when the students first settle in to model good behavior during independent work. Spend about five minutes writing and then begin your conferences. Make sure your students know what you are doing. You may decide to sit with them at a table, so that they see you. When students see you writing in a notebook, it helps to create a safe, close-knit atmosphere. Seeing you write makes students see you as part of their community, and it also gives their writing authenticity and real-world value.

Confer with Students:

The focus for today is to help students generate personal writing ideas. You might ask:

- *Are there any ideas on the chart you might like to try writing about today?*
- *Are there any entries in my notebook that you liked?*
- *What is important to you?*

Meet with students you have not met with yet. We have found that quiet students almost hide from the teacher during conferences. You'll want to make it clear that you will meet with every student at least once or twice a week.

You may need to help students come up with writing ideas. Have them refer to the list in the back of their writing notebooks again and try an idea they may not have thought of exploring.

Some of your students may be writing entries with just ten or twelve sentences. You may suggest that those students go back to a previous entry today rather than creating a new one. Consider teaching these students a technique we will visit in a later lesson. It's called "Stretching a Line," and it helps writers build around a single idea. Ask the student you are conferring with to reread the entry and choose a favorite sentence from it. The student then rewrites the sentence on a clean page and launches a new version of the old entry from that one sentence. Have them compare the new entry with the old one.

Reflect on the Day's Work/Share Our Ideas:

Signal the transition to share time.

I saw many of you writing in your notebooks. Who used this list of ideas to help them write today?

Show of hands. Try to get students who used the list to discuss how independent writing went for them today.

I'd really like to hear one or two new entries. Would someone like to share?

If time allows, you may want to share a new entry from your own notebook.

Before we leave for the day, I would like to discuss how I will be grading your writing. We know that by the end of these four weeks, we will be producing a final writing project. We know that there is a process we use to get there.

Refer to the Writing Cycle chart.

I want to remind you that you will receive a grade not only on the final project, but also a grade based on everything we do over the next four weeks. I will collect your notebooks once a week. You will receive a grade each week on your notebook work. Your notebook work includes all class work and homework. You will be responsible for keeping the notebook organized, so I can check it each week. I will check to make sure you have a date at the top of each entry.

Hand out copies of the Notebook Rubric. You may alter this rubric to suit the specific needs of your class. Review the rubric with your students.

We will have five Collecting lessons in total. We will be finished collecting by (give a date). Your notebook must be ready by this date.

Answer student questions.

Notebook Rubric

	1 below standards	2 approaching standards	3 meeting standards	4 [illegible] standards
Amount: Do I have the right number of entries? Did I write at least full page per entry?				
Use: Do I have different kinds of entries? Have I taken notes on mini-lessons?				
Thoughtfulness: Did I spend time on my entries?				
Presentation: Do I have the right headings? Are my entries dated?				

	1	2	3	4
Amount: Do I have the right number of entries? Did I write at least full page per entry?				
Use: Do I have different kinds of entries? Have I taken notes on mini-lessons?				
Thoughtfulness: Did I spend time on my entries?				
Presentation: Do I have the right headings? Are my entries dated?				

Follow-up:

- *For homework, students should write a new entry in their notebooks.*
- *Review the rubrics you'll expect to see in student notebooks when you collect them.*

Collecting Lesson #4: Personal Opinions

By the end of this lesson, students will:

- have begun to vary the types of entries they write in their notebooks;
- be familiar with the opinion/editorial genre;
- realize they have many opinions and can generate a great deal of writing around them.

Preparation:

1. Bring in a student editorial titled "Homework" to read aloud (see Appendix, p. 141).
2. Supply chart paper.
3. Create the chart called Opinion Sentence Starters (see p. 37).
4. Create the chart called Teacher's Completed Sentences (see p. 37).
5. Find three extra editorials of varying levels of difficulty to use in conferences. (These may be taken from daily newspapers or magazines, like *Muse* or *Sports Illustrated.*)

Introduce the Lesson:

In the lesson today, you will be reading an editorial to your students. We have provided a student sample for you, but you might want to find your own based on the needs and interests of your students. The article you choose should not be too difficult for them to understand. It may be helpful to provide handouts, so each student can follow along.

We know that we are still in the Collecting stage of the Writing Cycle, gathering many different writing ideas in our notebooks. *Refer to the Writing Cycle chart.* Today, I am going to show you another method for collecting writing in your notebook. It's a bit different from the other kinds of writing we have done so far. We are going to explore our opinions.

Teach the Lesson:

Eventually, we'll be publishing a finished writing project. It is important to think about the different kinds of writing that people publish before we even begin our drafts because that can direct the kind of writing we do. One kind of writing is nonfiction. Is anyone familiar with the word "nonfiction"? *Have a few students reply.* Nonfiction is based on fact—on real things and real events. One type of nonfiction is called editorial writing. Authors write editorials when they have an opinion about something currently going on in the world. Do you know what an opinion is?

Gather student ideas.

An opinion is a personal idea someone has about an event or another person or somebody's behavior. An opinion is not a fact. It is one person's own belief.

I have a student sample of an editorial that I'd like to read to you. It's called "Homework." As I read, think about the author's opinions.

Homework

I think homework is unfair. After a really long day at school, Teenagers just want to go home, watch some television and relax. We go to school from 8:00 A.M. to 3:00 P.M. That is most of our day! We study hard in school only to come home to more studying.

I also think homework makes no sense. What if there is no one at home to help you with homework? What if you didn't understand it in school and still don't understand it at home? Some parents work late and some don't speak English. How can they help us?

Kids deserve a break. We have other things that interest us. Many of us have dance classes after school and basketball games, swimming meets and other extracurricular activities to attend. Why do we have to give up doing what we love to extend the learning day into our personal lives?

Teachers put too much pressure on kids. Let us just be young while we have the chance. Let up on the homework. Please!!!!!

Read the article aloud.

What opinion was the author trying to communicate to us?

Responses may include: Homework is not fair, homework does not help students; homework is torture.

Notice that the author has strong opinions and backs up those opinions with evidence to support them.

Reread the author's assertion that homework rarely has helped him understand class work.

Transition to Independent Work:

I know that middle-school kids have LOTS of opinions about all kinds of things. The author of this article has a very strong opinion about homework. I'd like us to explore our opinions today, so that we can write an entry in our notebooks like this one.

Hang up the Opinion Sentence Starters chart.

OPINION SENTENCE STARTERS CHART

I think...

I feel...

I have a problem with...

I'm worried about...

I really like...

I made this chart to help us write our opinions. Write each of these sentence starters in your notebook. Leave about three lines in between each. Here is how I finished these sentences:

Hang up the Teacher's Completed Sentences chart. You can use the following sentences to help you write your own:

TEACHER'S COMPLETED SENTENCES CHART

I think pizza is delicious.

I feel unhappy when I see homeless people.

I have a problem with graffiti.

I'm worried about war.

I really like reality television shows.

I'd like you to take 15 minutes and finish these sentence starters in your notebooks.

When students are finished, choose three or four to share their opinions.

Now I'd like you to choose one of these sentences and write more about it in your writer's notebook. Choose the sentence you're going to explore and write it at the top of a new notebook page. Try to make your writing sound like the opinion writing we heard in the editorial called "Homework." You have about 40 minutes to write.

Signal the transition to independent work.

Confer with Students:

You may find that some students have not really found the voice of opinion writing. As you confer today, read from the extra editorials to help students who are having trouble finding the right tone. Have a discussion about the author's opinions and how he or she tries to convey them. Think about other genres by comparing the article to a text the student is familiar with. What are the differences?

Reflect on the Day's Work/Share Our Ideas:

Signal the end of independent work.

During share time, you may have students who do not wish to participate. We allow students in this situation to say, "Pass." Middle-school kids really value fairness. If they feel that you are pushing unjustly, they will not open up to the writing community. In order to make sure that everyone participates at some point, we came up with the rule that a student could pass only three times in the year. Most students use their passes wisely. Based on your teaching style and your class's personality, come up with your own rules.

What opinion did you write about today? Could I have a volunteer to read his or her entry? *Have students respond.* If you hear an opinion that you would also like to write about, please feel free to write it down.

Follow-up:

- *For homework, students should write about two more opinions.*
- *To reinforce this lesson, compare another kind of nonfiction text with the editorials.*

Collecting Lesson #5:
Using Literature for Writing Inspiration

By the end of this lesson, students will:
- have increased the variety of writings in their notebooks;
- have learned the Response to Literature genre;
- have learned another method of collecting writing in their notebooks.

Preparation:
1. Supply chart paper.
2. Write and review a Response to Literature entry in your own writer's notebook.
3. Review the first two chapters of *Toning the Sweep* by Angela Johnson (or another chapter book).

Introduce the Lesson:

We have found that this is a very useful lesson because it informally introduces students to a new genre while helping them collect more writing in their notebooks. Later in the year, you may choose to launch a formal genre study, but today you are simply exposing students to the Response to Literature as a tool for generating writing in their notebooks.

All of you have a good deal of writing in your notebooks. Take a minute and flip through your notebooks. Count how many entries you have. Turn to a partner and share the amount you have.

You may want to do the same

You should be really proud of yourselves. Some of you have almost twenty entries. I have been happy with how hard you have been working. Today is going to be our last day for collecting entries.

Point to the Writing Cycle chart.

The next time we meet, we will begin reviewing all the entries we have written in our notebooks and start making decisions about which ideas we want to develop further. So, I am going to finish Collecting with one last lesson—one more way for you to get as much writing in that notebook as you can before we start Choosing and Reflecting.

Point to the Writing Cycle chart.

Teach the Lesson:

We suggest you write off of a text like "Eleven" by Sandra Cisneros, but only if you have already shared that text with your students in the reading workshop.

You may choose to respond to that same text or use another. Whatever you decide, your students should already be acquainted with the text you respond to. We believe that the text you write about today should already be familiar to the students because the focus is not on deconstructing the text, but rather on writing off of a text.

Use the following language to help you discuss your own written response.

I am going to share an entry from my notebook that I wrote the day we read Sandra Cisneros's "Eleven." I kept thinking about that story and how unfair that teacher was to the little girl. It made me want to write and so I did. I was confused, though. I wasn't sure where to write. In my reading notebook? In my writing notebook? I decided to work in my writing notebook because this was my own reaction to the story—it wasn't a reading assignment.

Here's my entry:

Following you will find a sample entry to give you an idea of what an informal Response to Literature should look like. Share your own entry. When you are finished reading your response, ask students questions that will help them distinguish this kind of writing from the other kinds they have worked on so far.

SAMPLE RESPONSE TO "ELEVEN" BY SANDRA CISNEROS

After I read this story, I was angry. The teacher, Mrs. Price, was so mean to the little girl. She treated her unfairly. Who cares about an old sweater? Why was the teacher acting like it was such a big deal? I think the teacher was just picking on her.

I am a teacher and I don't know many kids who would put on an old, smelly sweater just because I told them to. But it would be cruel to try to make a child do that, especially in front of the entire class.

If Mrs. Price thought it was the little girl's sweater, she should have asked her privately, before lunch or after school. Mrs. Price should have believed the girl when she said it wasn't her sweater.

Whenever students leave sweaters or jackets in my wardrobe at school, I wait a few weeks for someone to claim the items. If they are still unclaimed, I give them to the school nurse, who makes sure kids who are in need get them.

Mrs. Price was careless and heartless. She publicly humiliated a little girl on her 11th birthday. She should not be a teacher.

What did you notice about my writing? How is it different from the other kinds of writing we have in our notebooks so far?

Your students may say, It's about a story we read; *or,* You wrote about a character; *or,* You wrote about your feelings about what the teacher did; *or even,* You wrote about an event that took place in a story, but the other entries in our notebook are not about a story.

You noticed the same things I noticed. My entry is called a Response to Literature. It is different from the other types of writing I have done so far because it is about a text I read. It is not a summary though; it is a reaction, a recording of my feelings about the story.

Let me share a new text with you today. When I am finished reading, I would like you to write a response to the text in your writer's notebook in the same way I did. I am going to read the first two chapters of an amazing story written by Angela Johnson called *Toning the Sweep*. This is a story about three generations of women, a grandma, a mother and a daughter, and how they come together to heal one another after they learn that their solid-as-a-rock grandma isn't so solid anymore. After I finish reading, you will all want me to finish the story!

Read aloud the first two chapters. This is a sensitive chapter dealing with the topic of child abuse. While it is not very graphic, it may make some kids sad. If you choose to use this text, please discuss the context of story before you read it and prepare children for what they will hear.

Transition to Independent Work:

I have so much I want to say about Grandma Ola and her role as a grandma to Emily. I know you want to tell me what you think of Gerald's mom or how you feel for the little boy. Don't tell. I know that you probably have many things to say about Ola and Diane's relationship and about Emily's relationship to Diane. Don't say anything. Write. You may choose to write about anything your mind is thinking about right this minute. Just write. Open your writer's notebooks and write. Just put that pen to your paper and go with it. This was a tough chapter. I am sure you have many emotions and feelings about what I just read to you. Find a space and begin. If you want to write about another book you have read, you may do so.

Signal the transition to independent work.

You may choose to let the students settle in for 10 minutes before you start conferring. During that time write in your own notebook in front of your students. You are a great model for them. When students see the teacher working with them, the writing community is enhanced.

Confer with Students:

Once students have begun to work, you should check your conference records to make sure you know whom you should confer with today. Be sure to confer with each student at least once weekly.

If you find that a student is having difficulty writing a response, perhaps you could reread a passage from Toning *to that child. Choose a paragraph or two that are likely to evoke an emotional response in the student. Have the student describe what he's feeling or thinks about the characters. If reluctant or blocked students talk to you about what they are feeling, they will most likely then be able to write a response.*

Reflect on the Day's Work/Share Our Ideas:

Signal the transition to share time.

How did it go for you today? Was it different writing about a published piece of writing?

Allow students to share their thoughts. It is always a good idea to find at least two volunteers ahead of time.

Would a few students like to share their responses?

This was our last collecting lesson for this study. The next time we meet, we will begin choosing an idea from our notebooks to explore in greater depth.

Follow-up:

- *For homework, students should write a response to the text they are currently reading independently.*
- *Consider ways your students can collect entries even while moving through the Writing Cycle toward publication.*

Looking Back and Looking Forward: Choosing a Topic

By the end of this lesson, students will:

- have moved forward in the Writing Cycle;
- have learned how to assess their notebook entries;
- have filled out the formal "Reflection" handout based on their writing experiences;
- have chosen one idea from their notebooks to explore further.

Preparation:

1. Supply copies of the "Writing Reflection" handout (see Appendix, pp. 142–143).
2. Review your notebook and mark entries for modeling reflection.
3. Fill out your own formal reflection.
4. Create a Choosing a Topic: Reflecting chart (see p. 45).
5. Create a Topic Idea Sign-up chart.

Introduce the Lesson:

This is a very layered lesson. You will be asking your students to reflect in their notebooks, fill out a formal questionnaire, and choose a topic from their notebooks for expanding into a publishable piece of writing. You might want to break it up. In our experience, it's good to give students at least a day to choose a topic. Even though this is a thirty-day lesson outline, you may choose to make it longer by extending any lessons you feel need to be broken up or revisited.

We've been working a lot in our notebooks, collecting many entries about all kinds of things. Today, we are going to move forward in the writing process to the second stage: Choosing.

Refer to the Writing Cycle chart.

During this stage, writers spend time reflecting, which means thinking very deeply, on all the different entries they have written, trying to find one idea they can take out of the notebook and spend a good deal of time working on, making it a bigger, more detailed piece of writing.

Teach the Lesson:

Hand out the "Reflection" sheet.

Today, I am going to ask you to choose a topic or idea from your notebook that you will explore further. In order to do this, you will need to spend time reflecting on your writing experience by rereading the entries in your notebooks. To help shape your thoughts about your notebook, I will also ask you to fill out the reflection form that I just handed out. It asks questions about your writing.

Choosing an idea in your notebook to possibly publish as a final piece is not as simple as picking your favorite entry. It takes time. One useful thing to do is look for ideas that flow throughout the notebook. Before you start, I want to share how I reflected on my notebook and how I finally came up with my topic.

Throughout the rest of the lesson, discuss how you arrived at your topic, using the following language as a guide:

I have been writing a lot in my notebook. I have so many entries that I decided it was time to do something with them. Last night, I began choosing a topic.

Refer to the Writing Cycle chart.

So I spent about 25 minutes rereading the entries in my notebook. You will notice that there are many sticky notes hanging out of the edges of my book. As I was rereading, I noticed that I wrote a lot about being in the third grade. So every time I read an entry that even mentioned being eight years old, I put a sticky note on that page. You will also notice that I folded some pages in half or turned down the corners of pages. Those pages are where I wrote opinion and fact entries, and I wanted to separate them from the other kinds of writing I did. Whenever an entry struck me as important or meaningful, like the one I wrote about pollution, I put a sticky note on it. Sometimes, if I liked it so much I didn't want to lose track of it, I made a big blue star at the top of it, like the one about my grandmother's chair. I folded the corner of one page because I liked just one sentence on the page about the third-grade dance festival we had when I was a kid. I highlighted that sentence. Basically, I want to be able to go back to those parts of my notebook that I really connected with, and in order to do that I leave little reminders, like sticky notes, stars in the margins, folded-down edges, and highlighted sentences.

Here is a chart that lists some reflection strategies I used that I thought might guide you while you are reflecting:

Name ______________________ Date ______________

Writing Reflection

1. What kinds of entries did you write in your notebook? (list the different kinds)
2. Do any topics appear in your notebook that you have written about before, maybe in another class or for another project? If so, list the topic or topics.
3. Are there any topics in your notebook that you never wrote about before? If so, list the topic or topics.
4. Which entry excites or puzzles or troubles or grabs you most? Why?
5. Which entries did you spend the most time working on?
6. Which entries did you spend the least time working on?
7. Which entries would you share with the class? Why?
8. Are there any entries that are similar? Do you write about a memory a few times in your notebook? Do you write about one topic over and over again? Do you write about one person a lot?
9. Are there any sentences that you wrote that stand out from the rest? Could you add more to these sentences to make new writing?
10. Remember, you are not choosing a favorite entry. You are choosing a topic to write about futher. You are choosing an idea. Right now choose two possible topic ideas from your notebook and discuss why you might choose them to develop in longer pieces of writing.

CHOOSING A TOPIC: REFLECTING

Underline a favorite entry.

Put a star next to a line that strikes you as important or beautiful.

Turn down the corner of a page of an entry that seems unfinished.

Notice topics that you repeat and place sticky notes on pages where they appear.

Note an entry or idea that could turn into a larger piece of writing.

Write notes to yourself, asking why you wrote things that stand out to you.

Fill out a formal reflection.

Review your formal reflection with your students. This will give them a clearer idea of what they are expected to accomplish. After you review the reflection, explain how you arrived at your topic. Make sure you do this by showing them both the notebook and the formal questionnaire.

I chose my topic idea based on what I noticed about my writing. I used my sticky notes, the markings in my notebook, and the reflection questions to help me choose the topic I wanted to write about. I had written about many things, so it was really hard to focus on just one thing. But when I paid attention, I noticed that I always wrote about the third grade or when I was eight years old. I asked myself why that topic was so important to me. I know that eight was a big year for me. For one thing, I went to a new school that year. I reread those entries again, and after discussing them with my friend, I realized that I had a lot to say about my teacher that year. All of my entries mention something about the classroom, the trips we took, or the things we learned. I realized that all of this had to do with Mrs. Jones, my third-grade teacher.

In our experience, having kids focus on the process by which they choose a topic really helps them think more deeply about their writing and the meanings behind it.

Transition to Independent Work:

The first thing I did in order to choose a topic was reflect. Refer to the Reflecting chart and spend about 25 minutes rereading and marking up your notebook. When you've finished that, you may begin the formal reflection sheet that I handed out earlier. Keep in mind that you are reflecting to choose a topic. Let's just go over the handout quickly to make sure you understand what I am asking you to think about.

Signal the transition to independent work. Let students know when 25 minutes are up and when they should start filling out the formal reflection.

Confer with Students:

Your main goal today is to have students discover the patterns or threads that flow throughout their writer's notebooks. You want them to look for concepts and preoccupations, not favorite entries. It would be helpful if you had your notebook available to review with students during conferences.

Reflect on the Day's Work/Share Our Ideas:

How many people found reflecting helpful? How about we go around the room and share some of our responses?

If you have not come up with your topic yet, it's okay. However, you should definitely work in your notebook tonight and confer with me tomorrow if you haven't already today.

Hang up a Topic Idea Sign-up chart. We like arranging this chart as a web: Write the words "Class Topics" in the center of the chart, then draw strands of the web, each one attaching to a student's name and topic. Invite students who have found their topics to sign up on the chart.

I'd like those of you who have found a topic to write your name and topic on this class chart, so that everyone has an idea of what their classmates are working on.

Follow-up:

- *For homework, students should write a paragraph in their notebooks about why they chose their topic.*
- *Collect the formal reflections from your students to use as an assessment tool.*

Nurturing Your Topic Idea: Making Lists

By the end of this lesson, students will:
- have moved to the third stage in the Writing Cycle.
- have generated more writing around their topics.

Preparation:
1. Review your notebook and mark items for modeling nurturing.
2. Display the Topic Idea Sign-up chart.
3. Create the Nurturing My Topic chart (see p. 48).
4. Post your entry written off a list on chart paper (see p. 48).

Introduce the Lesson:

By now, you are becoming aware of how we use the Writing Cycle. We have written lots of entries during Collecting, we all found topics during Choosing, and today we will begin Nurturing. When writers nurture their topic ideas, they basically write a lot more about them. When we collected entries, we wrote about many different kinds of things. When we nurture, we only write about one thing—our topic. Today, I am going to show you one strategy for generating more writing about your topic.

Teach the Lesson:

Use the following lesson as a guide to help you discuss how you generated more writing about your topic.

I told you that my topic idea is my third-grade teacher Mrs. Jones. We discussed how I came up with my topic. I had written about her a great deal in my notebook. I wasn't sure what more I could write about her. Then I thought of making lists, which has helped me find more ideas and details about my topics in the past. I opened up to a new page in my notebook and made a list of all the things that came to mind when I thought about Mrs. Jones. Here is my list:

NURTURING MY TOPIC: MRS. JONES

1. Smelled like strong perfume
2. Son's name was Andrew
3. Had a paralyzed arm
4. Made me feel bad because I was not good at math
5. Favored the popular kids
6. Waited with me when my mom was late after school
7. Danced with me to Michael Jackson's "Thriller" at the annual dance festival
8. Took us to the aquarium
9. Wore big glasses
10. Fell asleep at her desk in the afternoons

All of these things come to mind when I think of Mrs. Jones. Some of the things on my list describe what she looks like. Some are memories of her or memories I have because of her, like the aquarium trip. Now, I'd like everyone to stay at the meeting area. Open up to a clean page of your notebooks. Now you're going to make your own lists. Write your topic at the top of the page as I did. I want you to brainstorm words or groups of words that come to mind when you think of your topic. Go.

Give the students about 10 minutes to accomplish the task. Offer your support to those students who are having a difficult time making word associations.

Okay, time is up. You can finish your lists later. For now, I'd love to hear a few lists. First, tell us your topic to remind us of it and then share your list.

When you have heard about three students' lists you should move on.

The Nurturing stage of the Writing Cycle is when we develop our topics. So these lists are not enough. What I did next was choose one thing from my list that I wanted to write about. We can call this "writing off the list." I chose number ten—Mrs. Jones often fell asleep at her desk.

You should make sure the entry on your list is visible to all students.

Let me share my entry.

The following entry has been provided as a guide to help you understand what "writing off a list" looks like.

Nurturing My Topic: Mrs. Jones
#10 Asleep at Her Desk
I don't remember how many times it occurred in the school year, but I can safely say it was more than once that my third-grade teacher would rest her head on her desk during SRA time and conk out.

I don't really remember what SRA means, but it was the time of day when we would sit in groups according to color. (We all knew that your color was based on how well you could read.) Then you would go up to a box and take a story card and a question card. You would read the story and then

answer the questions. When you were finished, you'd return the cards to the box and take two more story and question cards. All the cards—the story card and question card—had group colors on them. I suppose that is how we third graders figured out that our color groupings were really reading groups based on reading level.

I remember Mrs. Jones would turn off the lights. SRA was always after lunch. Then she would lay her head on her desk and go to sleep while we worked. What astounds me most is that we actually worked! None of us misbehaved. What control that teacher had—even when she was sleeping we were well behaved.

I think it is weird that she slept. I am a teacher now and I would never fall asleep when students are in my room. Maybe that is why this memory is so alive in my head.

Transition to Independent Work

Take a minute and choose one thing off your list that you'd like to write more about. When you have found what you'll write about, put a star next to the number on your list. As I did, copy the item from your list onto a new page. When you have set up your page, you may find a place to write and begin.

Signal the transition to independent work.

Confer with Students:

We think you'll probably want to confer with those students who have very few items on their list. They may have an easier time generating a list if you let them think out loud with you. While they talk, you may want to jot down things they say that may inspire them to write later on.

Reflect on the Day's Work/Share Our Ideas:

I noticed so many of you really writing away today. I am very impressed. Who wrote a new entry off their list? Would you be willing to share your newest entry with the class? Before reading, it would be helpful if you explained what your topic is, just to remind us.

Follow-up:

- *For homework, students should continue this assignment at home. Give them a deadline by which they will be expected to have written five entries off their lists.*
- *To reinforce this lesson, have students continue this assignment in class the next day.*

Nurturing Your Topic Idea: Stretching a Line

By the end of this lesson, students will:
- know a new technique writers use to generate writing around one idea.

Preparation:
1. Bring your writing notebook.
2. Make handouts of your "writing off a list" entry used in the previous lesson.
3. Set up an overhead projector and write your "stretch" sentence on a fresh transparency.

Introduce the Lesson:

The last time we met as a writing group, we moved ahead in the Writing Cycle. Could someone point out where we are on the Writing Cycle chart?

Allow one student to point to the third stage of the Writing Cycle chart.

I see you guys are really getting acquainted with the writing process. That's right, we've reached the third stage, called Nurturing.

Teach the Lesson:

The sample dialogue presents the teacher's explanation of stretching a line about Mrs. Jones from her notebook. Use this to help you discuss how you stretched a line from your notebook.

Today I am going to introduce you to another strategy writers use in order to write more about a topic or idea. It is called "stretching a line."

Hand out copies of your entry.

I am handing out the entry I shared with you during our last writing session. I wrote this off my list about Mrs. Jones. You might remember that I chose #10, that Mrs. Jones would fall asleep at her desk. Let me read it to you again.

Read aloud.

You will notice that I highlighted one sentence in this entry:

Below is the last paragraph of the sample entry from the last writing lesson. The "stretch" sentence is in boldface.

#10 Asleep at Her Desk
I think it is weird that she slept. I am a teacher now and I would never fall asleep when students are in my room. Maybe that is why this memory is so alive in my head.

I highlighted the second sentence of this paragraph because it really stuck out in my mind. Out of all the sentences on the page, that one made me think the most. I knew I had more to say, so I took that sentence and rewrote it on top of a new page.

We find this a good opportunity to write in front of our students, letting them see—and believe—that writing is work for us, too. Seeing that you struggle to think of what to write next, that how you construct an entry is not very different from how they do it, will validate their efforts.

I am going to use this strategy to help me get more writing in my notebook about my topic, Mrs. Jones. I need you guys to be a bit patient with me today because I am going to write in front of you, and that is not easy. You will notice I took the sentence from my old entry and placed it on a new page. I will now use that entry to write more. Here goes.

Begin writing in front of your students. Think out loud when you are stuck. Show them that sometimes you cross out and start over. The following is an example of what stretching a line might look like:

I am a teacher now and I would never fall asleep when students are in my room. Not only is it rude and unprofessional, it's embarrassing! Teachers have a responsibility to their students to act as a role model and to instill a love of learning. If teachers fall asleep, what does that say about how they feel about learning? I also really feel that Mrs. Jones placed us in danger. While we mostly stayed seated out of fear she'd wake up, it was as if there were no adult supervision in the room.

Transition to Independent Work:

I would like you to stretch a line from your notebook. Make sure to choose a sentence from an entry that is about your topic! Spend about 10 minutes sitting here and rereading some of those entries. Look for a line that really stands out over all the others. Once you have found your sentence, circle or highlight it and then rewrite it on a new page. Make sure you title the page "Stretching a Line."

Choose two or three students to share the line they will stretch today. Then signal the transition to independent work.

When you are ready, you may move to independent writing.

Confer with Students:

This is another opportunity to talk to kids about their topic choices. If students aren't able to find anything else to say, help them see that they may not have chosen a good topic to write about. Let them know: A good topic holds your attention—you will want to write a lot more about it; a good topic allows you to write a great deal about it; a good topic comes out of the notebook—it is not just one favorite entry but is a string of ideas and thoughts that runs through several entries. Explain that when we notice such a string in our own writing, we are finding something that is very important to us.

Reflect on the Day's Work/Share Our Ideas:

How many people were able to stretch a line today? Was it a helpful way to gather more writing in your notebook?

Ask three or four students to share their thoughts. As in your conferences today, it may be a good idea to review what makes a good topic.

Follow-up:

- *For homework, students should lift another line from their notebooks and stretch it.*
- *To reinforce this lesson, make A Good Topic chart and review it again with the class.*

Drafting: Planning and Mapping

By the end of this lesson, students will:

- have organized their notebook in terms of whether entries will or will not be included in their first draft.
- have begun writing their first drafts.

Preparation:

1. Prepare a class set of sample first, second, third, and final drafts (see Appendix, pp. 144–149).
2. Create the How to Write a First Draft chart (see p. 56).
3. Supply drafting folders for each student.
4. Display five to ten texts students are familiar with from past mini-lessons, varying in genre.
5. Create transparencies of your draft map from your notebook, along with the first draft. Alternatively, create class sets of the map and draft.

Introduce the Lesson:

This is a very intense lesson that relies heavily upon modeling your thinking as you created a first draft. We encourage new teachers to spend two or three days on it. Read it over and decide where you could turn this one lesson into two or three separate lessons depending upon the strengths of your students.

We have all chosen our topics, and we've nurtured them by developing their ideas in our notebooks. Today is a very important day in the writing workshop because we are moving forward in the Writing Cycle to the fourth stage, called Drafting.

Refer to the Writing Cycle chart.

Drafting is a very big deal for writers because this is the time when we begin writing outside of the notebook. This is the point in the Writing Cycle when we imagine what our finished project will be like out of the notebook, in its published form. And it's when we writers organize our notebook selections and take words and phrases and sentences and ideas from them to use in writing the new piece. This new piece will be the first version of our final piece. This first version is called the "draft." Drafting is when we begin writing on loose-leaf paper and keeping our work in drafting folders.

Teach the Lesson:

Hand out the student sample packets

I am handing out a sample of a student's writing project, so you can see what drafts of writing look like. Today we're concentrating on first drafts, but I also want you to get an idea of what second and final drafts look like. All three drafts have some things in common, but each draft is also different from the others. You'll notice that the front page is a first, or rough, draft. If you flip two pages you will see a second draft. This student even made a third draft. Finally, you will notice a very clean, polished piece of writing. That is called the final draft. Take a few minutes and flip through the packet with someone next to you. See if you can locate similarities and differences among the drafts. What do you find?

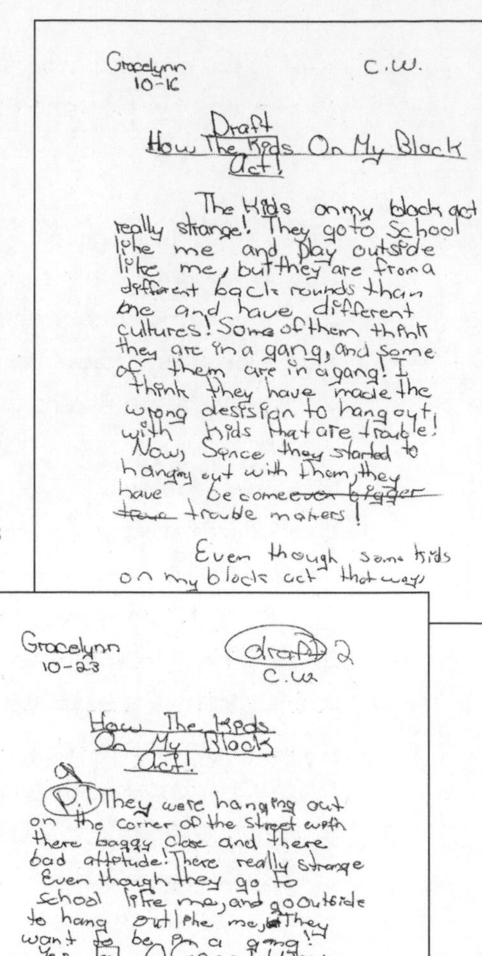

Gracelynn 10-16 C.W.

Draft

How The Kids On My Block Act!

The Kids on my block act really strange! They go to School like me and play outside like me, but they are from a different backrounds than me and have different cultures! Some of them think they are in a gang, and some of them are in a gang! I think they have made the wrong desisan to hang out with kids that are trouble! Now, since they started to hanging out with them, they have become even bigger have trouble makers!

Even though some kids on my block act that way

Gracelynn 10-23 draft 2 C.W.

How The Kids On My Block Act!

P.1 They were hanging out on the corner of the street with there baggy close and there bad attitude! There really strange Even though they go to school like me, and go outside to hang out like me, they want to be in a gang! Yes A Gang? Why would somebody want to be a bad person? I know I wouldn't!!!

P.2 I think they have made the wrong decsion! Before they have started to hang out with them, they were good kids. But when they

Students should notice that the genre, topic, and structure remain the same from draft to draft, and that some sentences even remain the same. They should also notice that the final draft is a clean copy. They may notice that the introductory paragraph has been significantly altered or that many sentences have been changed or moved around, and that sentences have been deleted from the first draft.

I am sharing this student work with you to give you a sense of the big picture. I want you to understand that the first draft is not a final project. It is your first try. By the time you publish a final draft, you will have made many changes to your first draft, just as the student who wrote this work did.

So what do we do first? How do we plan for our own drafts? First, we have to think about what we want to publish. It is important to envision the final project because that helps guide us. It is kind of like having a road map: If we don't know where we are going, the map is useless. If we don't have an idea about how this project will look when completed, we won't know what to do to get there.

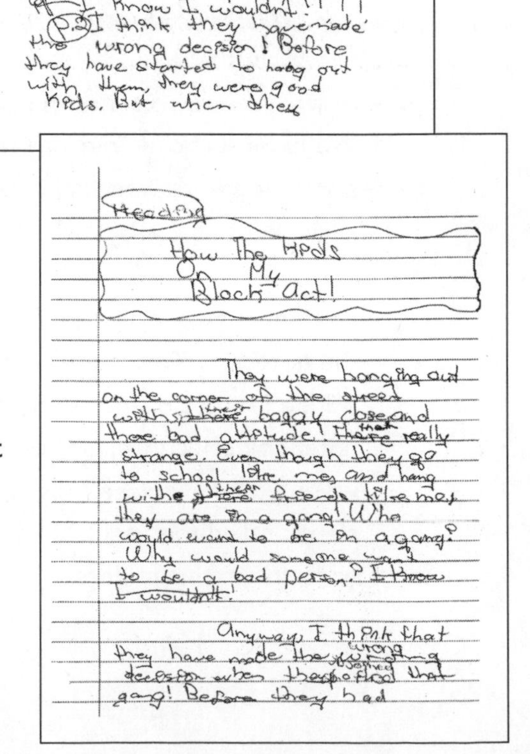

Heading

How The Kids On My Block Act!

They were hanging out on the corner of the street with their baggy close and their bad attitude! They really strange. Even though they go to school like me, and hang with their friends like me, they are in a gang! Who would want to be in a gang? Why would someone want to be a bad person? I know I wouldn't!

Anyway, I think that they have made the wrong decsion when they joined that gang! Before they had

Think about all the texts we have read in class so far. *Point to a display of texts read so far.* We have read nonfiction articles, a short story, picture books, and memoirs. I am going to leave these works on this table for you to look at for the rest of meeting time today, and they'll be here for the rest of the week for you to use as references. And, of course, any kind of writing you've ever read can serve as your model, so ask yourself which kind of writing you are most interested in publishing. Will you publish a memoir? Will you publish a nonfiction article, like a feature in a newspaper or magazine? Will you publish a collection of poems? Will you publish a fiction picture book or a nonfiction picture book?

Here is a sample discussion about making drafting decisions. You should use this example as a guide for how to think aloud with your students:

When I was figuring out how my writing would best be published, I thought about my topic, Mrs. Jones. How should I write about Mrs. Jones? Well, not nonfiction because even though she is real, I'm not writing facts about her; I'm describing my memories. I thought of Sandra Cisneros's *House on Mango Street*, which is a collection of vignettes, or short descriptions, that tell one main story by describing many small memories. I decided I would write vignettes about Mrs. Jones. After I decided how my writing would be published, I had to figure out how to get there.

So the first thing I did was reread everything I had written about Mrs. Jones, and I used a highlighter to mark every sentence I really wanted to be sure I included in my draft.

Show students your notebook and the places where you highlighted something about your topic.

I had to leave behind many sentences in the notebook, and that was really hard to do. I even had to share some of my entries with my husband and get his advice. After I figured out what pieces of writing I wanted to use in my draft, I had to organize them. I had sentences and paragraphs from many different entries, and the draft would never make any sense if I had just copied everything right out of the notebook the way it was. So I had to arrange the writing I was going to use—I had to figure out what would come first, second, third, and so on.

I opened a clean page in my notebook and wrote "Draft Map" at the top.

Show students the Draft Map page in your notebook.

My map is a web. I drew a circle at the center of the page and wrote "Mrs. Jones" in it. Then I drew branches on the web. I flipped back through my notebook and found the writing I wanted to include about her falling asleep at her desk. On one strand of the web I wrote, "Slept at her desk." Then I flipped to the paragraph about her being mean to me about my math skills. On a strand of the web I wrote, "Math story." I found five things that I wanted to write about, and I added them to the map.

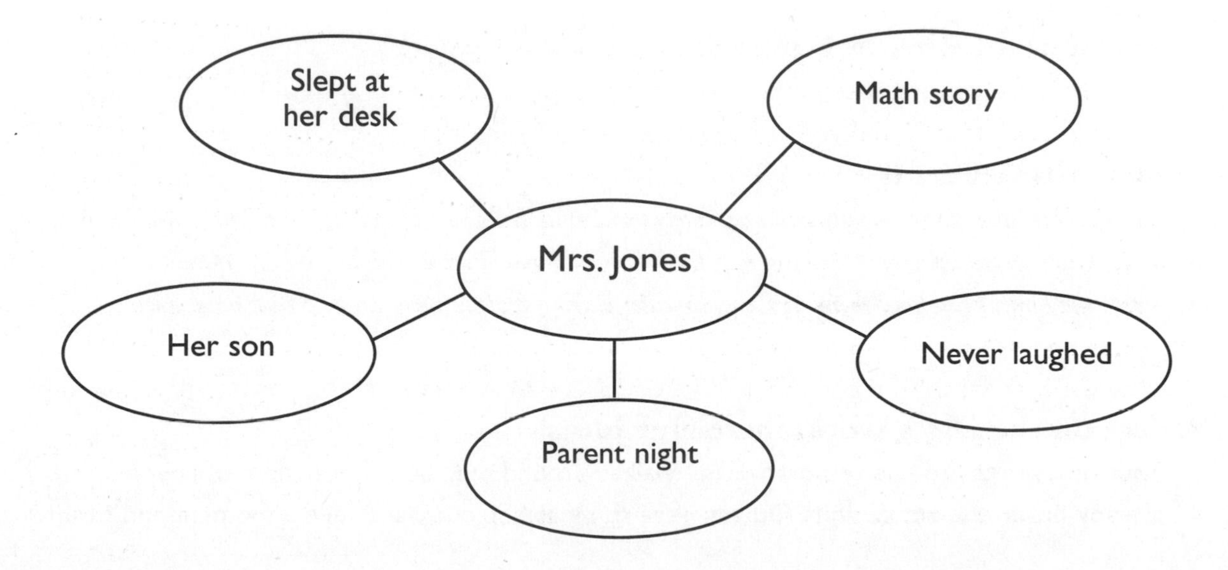

Finally, I had to decide the order in which these strands would show up in my writing, so I numbered them. Then I started writing off my map. I sat down with my notebook, my map, and a piece of paper and began. I included all the writing I had chosen in my notebook, and I also added some new stuff. This is my first draft:

Read your first draft to your students. You may consider giving out copies also.

Transition to Independent Work:

Now it's your turn to get started. I know this was a very big lesson today. Do your best and remember, I will be here to help you. Here is a chart about drafting that I thought might help guide you:

HOW TO WRITE A FIRST DRAFT

1. **Decide what you want the final, published piece to be like—what genre will it be?**
2. **Examine familiar texts for publishing ideas.**
3. **Reread your notebook and highlight the best sentences about your topic.**
4. **Talk with a partner about your sentence choices.**
5. **Create a map of your draft.**
6. **Decide the order of the items on your map and number them.**
7. **Write you first draft on loose-leaf paper.**

Maybe we could have some volunteers discuss how they are going to get started today.

Have students share.

Signal the transition to independent work.

If you feel ready to begin, go ahead. If you would like to stay at the meeting area for some extra support, feel free to do so and I'll help you.

Confer with Students:

A great deal of your conferring today will most likely be with students who cannot organize their ideas. Review how to use the map as a graphic organizer. You may find that some students need you to go through their entries with them and create the Draft Map with them. You may consider pairing students who can help each other create their webs.

Reflect on the Day's Work/Share Our Ideas:

Your first drafts are due tomorrow. As I walked around the room, I noticed most people had already begun the actual draft. Others were still mapping out plans. Take a moment and turn to a partner to discuss your plan of action for tonight. What do you need to do when you get home to complete your first draft?

Students should share their plans with one another and then the larger group can discuss them.

Follow-up:

- *For homework, students should complete the first draft.*
- *To reinforce this lesson, you may need to repeat what you taught today. Take your cue from the drafts students hand in. Use what you notice about the drafts to come up with lessons for your next writing study.*

Revising: Writing New Leads

By the end of this lesson, students will:

- have moved forward in the Writing Cycle to Revising;
- understand how revision works;
- understand the function of the lead.

Preparation:

1. Supply copies of the "Five Kinds of Leads" handout (see Appendix, p. 151).
2. Revise your own first draft, marking the page with directions, such as arrows, cross-out lines, insertion carrots, and so on.

Introduce the Lesson:

I read over all of your drafts and will be handing them back to you today. I am impressed by your efforts. I really learned so much about each of you as writers. When you get back your work, read the individual comments I wrote.

Hand back drafts.

Today we will move forward in the Writing Cycle. *Refer to the Writing Cycle chart.* We will move into the stage called Revising. When we revise, we look at our drafts to see where we can make changes to them. We look at our sentences and words and we think about changes that can make our writing sound better and be as understandable as possible. We don't look at spelling or paragraphs or neat handwriting or run-on sentences. We will look at those things later, when we edit.

Refer to the Writing Cycle chart.

There are many, many different ways to revise writing. Over the course of the school year, we will look at several techniques. For now, I am going to share one revising strategy that, based on your drafts, I think will help you. I noticed, in general, that your leads could use some work. So today we'll take a look at them and see if we can make some smart changes.

Teach the Lesson:

A lead is the first sentence or group of sentences at the beginning of a written work. The lead is important because it is the first glimpse of your writing that a reader gets to see. The lead actually *leads* the reader into the rest of the piece. If the lead is not catchy or interesting, the reader might not continue reading the rest your work. I don't mean that every lead needs to start off with action words, like WOW! POW! BOOM! There are many ways to catch a reader's attention without overdoing it. There are many different types of leads, and they suit different kinds of writing. Let's take a look at this handout.

Read the "Five Kinds of Leads" handout. Discuss the five different types of leads. A discussion of this handout could begin like this:

Here is a chart that shows five different kinds of leads that an author might use to begin his or her writing. There are more than five leads an author can use, but for the sake of today's work, I have decided to show you five leads that you might want to use. The first lead is called the action lead. This is a really good lead for fiction or narrative writing. The author starts the piece in the middle of the story—right where the action is—before telling the reader what has already happened. It really grabs the reader's attention.

Continue discussing the five kinds of leads.

Five Kinds of Leads

(Remember: The lead should grab your reader's attention.)

1. Action—The reader is immediately drawn into the action of the story.

I heard a loud crash, my little brother [illegible] and I [illegible]. When I got to the backyard, blood was everywhere and Michael was sitting holding his knee, crying. Pieces of broken bottle lay in the blood pooling around him. I began to panic.

2. Dialogue—The text begins with one or more people speaking.

"Jason! Jason, help me!"

I ran out the kitchen door to the backyard, where my bother was playing. When I got there, I knew it was bad.

"Are you...? Are you..."

That was all I could say. Nothing else would come out of my mouth.

3. Setting—This traditional beginning describes time and place.

One Saturday night during the summer, my parents decided to go to a movie. I was in charge of my little brother Michael, and I was in a bad mood. I didn't want to baby-sit on Saturday night. Michael was much younger than I and really annoying. He always got into my stuff and asked too many questions while I watched television.

4. One-Sentence Wonders—The opening paragraph is only one sentence long, and it's provocative.

I will never forgive myself for what happened to Michael.

5. Reflection—The narrator examines the subject, describing thoughts and feelings.

I never appreciated my little brother Michael. I thought he was annoying, a nuisance, a burden. But that horrible night I learned how important he is to me. I realized I would do anything for Michael. Anything.

Transition to Independent Work:

Turn to a partner and talk about what kind of lead you might use in your draft.

Give students five minutes for a brief discussion.

You should try revising your draft by writing three new leads today. Think about what kinds of leads you would like to try. After you experiment writing new leads, pick the one you want to add to your first draft.

Before you go, I want to show you how to change the lead on your actual draft. There are many ways to do this. The most important thing to remember is that you never use white-out or an eraser on you drafts. I always want to see what you had written before you made the change. So you can cross out the old lead and write the new one in the margins or at the top of the page. Or you can write the new lead on a new piece of paper, cut it out, and staple it over the old lead. Make sure you only staple one side so that I can lift the scrap of paper and see the old lead.

Use your first draft as a visual aid as you discuss revision marks. Signal the transition.

Confer with Students:

Some students may be done very quickly. If so, ask them to try writing more than three different leads. You could also have them look through some of the books in the library they have already read. Can they identify the kinds of lead the authors used?

Other students may feel stumped. While we have found that most students publish narratives or memoirs in the first writing study, you will have a few students who do not. If they aren't writing a narrative piece, it may be hard to use an action lead. Discuss leads that are appropriate for the specific genre they are publishing.

Reflect on the Day's Work/Share Our Ideas:

What kinds of lead did you try? First share your old lead and then share the new one.
Have students share their new leads.

Follow-up:

- *For homework, have students change the lead of a past notebook entry.*
- *To reinforce this lesson, ask students to identify the kinds of leads used by a selection of authors, perhaps from their independent reading books.*

Revising: Cutting and Adding

By the end of this lesson, students will:
- know more about Revising;
- have focused their first drafts by cutting writing that doesn't belong;
- have added to their drafts.

Preparation:
1. Supply copies of the student narrative sample titled "Visiting" (see Appendix, p. 152).
2. Create the Revising: Cutting & Adding chart (see p. 62).

Introduce the Lesson:

Yesterday we moved into the Revising stage of the Writing Cycle. We looked at our leads and made changes to them to grab the reader's attention. Today we are going to continue revising our first drafts.

Teach the Lesson:

Cutting and adding is very difficult for students. It will take practice for them to develop an eye for what is superfluous or repetitive and what is missing. Don't be surprised if your students are very reluctant to delete their own words.

Another technique writers use to revise their work is known as "cutting." Very often as we write, we add lots of information that does not need to be there. We do this because as we write, our minds take us to many different ideas all at once. Or we have so much to say that we fill the page with too much information. That's okay for a first draft. But now it is time to cut out what doesn't belong. Let's take a look at this student's writing and see if we can cut out extra words or sentences that don't seem to belong in the story.

Hand out "Visiting."

As I read, pay attention to what this narrative is mostly about.

Visiting—Draft #1

I woke up at about 5am when my alarm clock rang. Beep. Beep. I didn't want to get up I was so tired. But I knew today was my big day to go visit my dad in Delaware. I got up and went to the kitchen and ate breakfast with my mom. I ate some cereal and then got dressed. When I was ready my mom said "come on Benny we are gonna be late". So, we left and we took the train to the bus station. Their were many people in the train station so many I felt trapped. I waited with my mom for the bus and then kissed her goodbye. I couldn't wait to visit my Dad in Delaware. The bus was crowded and I listened to my walkman the whole way. It was a long ride. I ate the lunch my mom packed for me. I ate a sandwich and soda and chips. I looked out the window and saw lots of cars and big green signs. We went over a very big, wide bridge. I was sad because I already missed my mom.

The bus finally got to Delaware and when I got off the bus I saw my aunt and two cousins waiting for me. I hugged my aunt and said hi to my cousins and then we got in her car and drove to my dad's house. I gave my dad a hug and then we went out to eat to Red Lobster. The next day my aunt and two cousins took me to the movies and then I slept at her house for a slumber party.

We had so much fun. I really loved being in Delaware with my dad. When I came home I was happy to see my mom but sad to leave my dad and aunt.

Read text aloud.

The following is a sample dialogue about this text:

TEACHER: What was the student's topic? What was the main idea of the narrative?

STUDENT A: His family.

TEACHER: Well, yes, he does write about his family. But is his purpose in writing this narrative to tell you all about his family? Or is the author trying to tell you about something else?

STUDENT B: It's about visiting his family because the title is "Visiting."

TEACHER: Very good. The title lets us know what this piece should be about. Notice I said, "should." Do you think that the author has done a good job telling us about a visit with his family? This student has included lots of information. But does he tell us much about the actual visit?

STUDENT C: It seems like the whole first page is about getting there. He talks about waking up and then the bus ride. He hardly tells about the visit to Delaware.

TEACHER: I'm glad you caught that. While the author may have remembered waking up that morning and had the memory of the bus ride on his mind, was it really necessary to add this to the draft? Does that information help us understand what he did in Delaware?

STUDENT D: I think he can get rid of that. It doesn't belong.

TEACHER: I agree. Cutting out our words can often be very hard to do. But as writers, we sometimes need to take chances to make our work as good as it can be. If we leave in information that is unnecessary, then we will just have a lot of unfocused writing. If we get rid of the stuff that doesn't belong, then our writing will be interesting to our readers, and it will successfully communicate our ideas. Our writing will be clearer and our story will seem vivid and important.

If the author cut the first paragraph, the piece would start at the second paragraph, which begins: "The bus finally got…" But he would then need to think about "adding"—he would need to flesh out the rest of his piece. He could say more about the actual visit because the piece seems incomplete without information about his father and his aunt. He never tells us what he did in Delaware or what Delaware is like. He could write about things his father said to him or places they visited together.

I shared this student sample with you because I wanted you to get an idea of what cutting and adding means. Let's look at this revising chart:

REVISING: CUTTING & ADDING

Reread your writing.

Find the focus—What are you really writing about?

What doesn't belong? What sentences have nothing to do with your topic?

Where could you add more about your topic?

What could you add to flesh out your topic?

Transition to Independent Work:

Use this chart to help you cut out what doesn't belong in your writing. I know this isn't easy to do. You will need to think about your words carefully. Remember that this student added too much information, and that was unnecessary. The extra information about the bus ride did *not* make the piece better. But also remember that we thought after cutting the extra stuff, it would have been good to add details about his actual visit with his father and his aunt. What changes can you make in your own piece to make it clearer, fuller, more interesting?

Remember that after you cut sentences, you may have to add to your work to get at the heart of what you really want to say.

Signal the transition to independent work.

Confer with Students:

You should spend time with students who are struggling with cutting and adding. Walk them through the steps: have them identify the topic of their piece, then help them identify superfluous passages. You may want to read a student's piece to her. Sometimes when they hear it, they are able to identify what is not needed.

If you find some students do not need to cut words, have them focus on adding.

Choose a few students who will discuss their conferences with you during share time.

Reflect on the Day's Work/Share Our Ideas:

Signal the transition to share time.

I walked around and saw many of you working hard on your drafts. I had some very good conferences with some of you about the changes you have decided to make to your work. Could my volunteers share what we discussed?

Have students share what was discussed in the conferences.

Follow-up:

- *For homework, students should write a second draft, continuing to cut and add. They should bring their work to the next class.*
- *Spend another class revising by showing students how to create a second draft based on their cuts and additions. (For information about the second draft, see the following lesson.)*

Editing: Editing Partnerships

By the end of this lesson, students will:

- have formed peer editing partnerships;
- know how to conduct themselves with their partners;
- know what to discuss with their partners;
- understand the difference between revising and editing.

Preparation:

1. Supply copies of student nonfiction sample titled "Dog Care" (see Appendix, p. 153).
2. Create a blank chart titled Editing Ideas (see p. 65).
3. Create the How to Edit with a Partner chart (see p. 66).

Introduce the Lesson:

Yesterday we worked on revising our first drafts. Today you should all have a clean second draft. The second draft has all your changes on it and looks very different from the first draft. In what ways?

Students might respond: "The lead grabs the reader's attention," or "unnecessary words and sentences were cut and more writing added."

Don't throw out your first drafts. You will need them because I'm going to collect them with your final project. Keep them in your folder.

Today we are going to begin editing our work. *Refer to the Writing Cycle chart.*

Editing is very different from revising. When we revised, we changed the ideas of the text—the big things. We moved sentences and played with words to make our writing more detailed and focused, and to make it sound better. We studied our sentences and made sure they made sense for the reader. When we were revising, we didn't look at the spelling or the punctuation. Now it's time to do that.

Teach the Lesson:

In this lesson, you will give students a chance to show you what they already know about grammar and editing. Since the main purpose of the lesson is to accustom students to working in partnerships, you will not teach one specific editing technique. Rather, you will gather ideas from students about what they should look for when reviewing each other's work. As you discuss editing, fill in the Editing Ideas chart. This way students will be equipped to work independently and you will be able to assess what they know. This informal assessment will allow you to create grammar and editing lessons that specifically address your students' needs.

The editing stage is important because this is where you take control of your own work. This is where you really need to think about the reader. The reader depends on you to give them the right directions. Your punctuation tells your reader how fast to read a passage, indicating when to stop, when to pause, when to hurry on. It also controls your meaning. Now that we're in the Editing stage, we will review these symbols, including how and when to use them.

What do you know about editing already? Take some time, turn and talk to a partner, and together make a list of all the different ways you know how to edit. Talk about what you know about grammar and punctuation. Talk about what you make sure you do to your writing before you hand it in to be graded—and to make it ready for publication!

Give students some time to work in the meeting area. Walk around and facilitate these conversations.

Okay. Let's fill in our Editing Ideas chart.

Begin a discussion about grammar and punctuation. Students may know a great deal and, therefore, you will have a big list. Or they may not have a solid background in editing skills and the list may be short. In the middle grades, students should know:

EDITING IDEAS

Correct spelling.

Use a period at the end of a sentence.

Start each sentence with a capital letter.

Let's get some more ideas for our chart.

Hand out student sample titled "Dog Care."

This is a sample of a nonfiction draft. It is about taking care of your dog. It is a part of a bigger research report about dog care. This student struggled with editing. I thought we could look at one page from her report to get editing ideas for our own drafts.

Read the text aloud. Make sure you read it with the grammatical flaws. You should probably read it twice. Slow down where it's choppy or there's a fragment. Quicken the pace when you hit a run-on. If you allow your students to read this to themselves, they may not see the problems. However, in our experience, students will notice that something is wrong with the lead when they hear the fragment, "If you had a dog." They know that something has been left unsaid.

Have a conversation about the piece. Your conversation may sound like this:

TEACHER: There are problems in the first few sentences of this text. Did anyone hear anything strange?

Dog Care

If you have a dog. Dogs need to be taken good care of. They need to be washed a lot and fed all the time. Dogs need to be walked and need to have a place to play and a place to sleep. They need a comfortable place to lay down. you have to always watch out for your dog and make sure it don't get hit by a car. Also when you have a dog you take the dog to a animal doctor called a veterinarian. You should love your pet and give it a good home and brush his fur everyday so that he doesn't shed too much in the house. Also if you have little kids in your house you should watch out for the dog could bite the little kids. If you play too rough. Sometimes, people sneeze from dogs and then you have to give them away. But not if you brush the dog everyday then you can stop him from shedding too much. I have a dog and I love him very much and I take good care of him. Do you take care of your dog?

STUDENT A: The first sentence sounded weird.

TEACHER: What do you mean by "weird"?

STUDENT A: It doesn't make sense. "If you have a dog." If you have a dog, what? It's like the author forgot to finish the sentence.

TEACHER: Oh! I see what you are saying. You mean the first sentence is just a part of a sentence. We call that a fragment. A fragment is a group of words that does not make a complete thought. Let's add the word "fragment" to our editing chart.

You should decide ahead of time how long you'll discuss "Dog Care." You may wish to generate at least one or two more ideas for the editing list. Stay general about each editing idea the students present. You will get more specific as the year unfolds.

You are going to use our Editing Ideas chart today. When we edit, it is often very hard to see our own mistakes. After all, you have spent a great deal of time reading and rereading your work. If you had noticed an error, you would have corrected it already! Our eyes sometimes skip over our own mistakes because we know what we mean to say. This is why we often work in editing partnerships. Has anyone ever worked with a peer editor before?

Hold a brief discussion about student experiences.

I am going to allow you to choose your partner for today. If I feel you made an unwise choice, I will make a change.

In this lesson, we usually allow students to choose their own partners. However, we have also chosen partners before the lesson and posted the groups on a chart. Sometimes letting children choose their own partners results in a few students feeling left out. However, when you choose for your students, you indicate that you doubt their ability to make wise choices. Both ways can work; it depends on the maturity level of the students. You should decide what works for you and your classroom.

Before you choose partners and go to work, I'd like to share my expectations with you about how you will work with your partner. Can someone read the chart aloud?

Choose a volunteer. Stop at each expectation to discuss in greater detail. Here is a sample chart:

HOW TO EDIT WITH A PARTNER

1. Sit knee to knee on the rug or across from one another at desks.
2. Keep eye contact with your partner.
3. Have your drafts in front of you.
4. Use your drafts to make conversation.
5. Stay on task—conversation should be about drafts, not about lunch time.
6. Suggest ways your partner can edit his or her draft.
7. Always start with a positive comment about your partner's work.
8. When you think your partner needs to make an editing change, use phrases like: "This is good, but I think it would sound better if..." or "I think that your sentence is catchy, but..."
9. Consider your partner's editing advice even if you do not follow it.

Transition to Independent Work:

Take a minute and choose a partner. You may work with only one other person. If you need a partner, I'll help set you up.

If there is an odd number of students in your class, allow one group of three. Signal the transition.

It would be great if you could observe your students and take notes on how they are working together. You may need to remind some about staying on task or about their body language. Listen to the conversations. What are students saying? Do they know how to offer advice? Are they too critical? Is the editing chart helping them?

Confer with Students:

Since students are working in partnerships, you will probably hold group conferences today. Your discussion could begin by having students discuss the effectiveness of working with a partner. Have the partners talk to you about the ways they are helping one another.

If you have two students in a struggling partnership, have them observe a successful one. You could also model working together by joining them for a few minutes.

Reflect on the Day's Work/Share Our Ideas:

Signal the transition to share time.

How did it go for you today? What was it like working with a partner?

Listen to student responses.

Follow-up:

- *For homework, students should write a reflection on what it was like to work with a partner.*
- *To reinforce this lesson and model the editorial partnership, ask two students who worked well together to have a conversation about it in front of the class. They may need some direction.*

Editing: Writing in Paragraphs

By the end of this lesson, students will:
- know how to use paragraphs;
- understand the Editing stage of the Writing Cycle;
- have continued building editing partnerships.

Preparation:
1. Supply copies of the Writing in Paragraphs handout (see Appendix, p. 154). You may also want to display a copy on chart paper or the overhead.
2. Create the Writing in Paragraphs chart (see below).
3. Bring a text with paragraphs that students are familiar with from Reading Workshop (for conferring).
4. Optional: Retype a text without paragraphs. Use one that students know well from Reading Workshop (for conferring).

Introduce the Lesson:

Yesterday, we worked in peer editing partnerships to begin editing our second drafts. We came up with a list of editing ideas. Today, I will focus on one editing technique that I think is very important for you. I want to look at paragraphs, why we use them, and how we use them.

Teach the Lesson:

When you write in paragraphs, you organize your thoughts for the reader. Paragraphs allow the reader to follow your ideas by presenting those ideas in neat sections. Here are the rules for writing in paragraphs:

WRITING IN PARAGRAPHS

1. **Begin a new paragraph every time you switch to a new idea, thought, or subject.**
2. **In a dialogue—a conversation between two or more people or characters—begin a new paragraph each time the speaker changes.**

I am going to help you understand writing in paragraphs by sharing some writing with you that is *not* in paragraph form. Let's look at the first text, Sample 1, together.

Distribute the handout.

You will notice that this writing is not in paragraph form. If it were in paragraph form, the text would be divided into indented sections.

Hold up a copy of a text that is properly written in paragraph form.

Like this text: Notice that the author every so often begins a new sentence a few spaces into the line. This is called indenting. Every time the author begins a new subject or thought he begins a new paragraph. He begins the next sentence on a new line and starts writing about one thumbprint into the line.

Writing in Paragraphs

SAMPLE 1

When I grow up I want to be a veterinarian. A veterinarian is an animal doctor. I love animals and that is why I want to help take care of them when I am older. I know you have to go to school for a long time to be an animal doctor. You have to have a degree from high school, college and veterinary school. You also need to have high grades and intern in an animal hospital before you can own your own practice. When I own my practice, it will be in Brooklyn because that is where I am from. There are a lot of animals that need love in Brooklyn like stray cats and dogs. I want to help give these lost animals check ups and homes. I will never charge a fee for an animal brought in from the street without a home. Whoever brings those animals in should be thanked not charged. My dog is named Jake and I love him. He is a black mixed Labrador and he is the reason I decided to become a Vet.

SAMPLE 2

When mama got home from work, she was exhausted. I asked her, "Mama, can I have money for my school trip?" Mama hardly looked at me as she mumbled to herself and threw her tired body onto the couch. "Baby, rub mama's feet, then we'll talk money." I hated rubbing her feet. I was the only one in the house who ever did it. Would Johnny? My brother was too wrapped up in himself and Papa didn't get home until after bedtime. Mama worked hard on her feet all day at a grocery store. I felt bad asking her for money and I felt bad that she had hurt feet. As I sat on the floor, I massaged her feet as she told me about her day. "Mr. Jones really did it today. He was so rude to me in front of a customer." I grew red with anger. "What did he say to you; mama?" I carefully worked my thumbs into her soles. Mama answered, "He told me I was lazy and worked too slowly." Mama looked sad. I knew she was one of his best workers but when Mr. Jones was in a bad mood he took it out on Mama. Papa always tells her to quit, "Sandra, quit that job, we'll make do." But Mama won't quit. She knows how hard Papa works already. "I have a growing girl who needs things," Mama always responds. Mama wanted me to have all that she didn't.

The first piece I will read is about one student who wants to become an animal doctor. It is not written in paragraph form.

When reading, you should exaggerate the lack of paragraphs by rambling. You want students to notice that all of the sentences are mashed together.

What did you notice about how I read this text?

Students should respond: "You read too fast," or "You didn't take a breath," or "You made it hard to understand."

This is a well-written nonfiction essay. Maybe we could help this author edit her work by putting it into paragraph form. Let's do it together. I will read it out loud again. When you think the author should have begun a new paragraph, let me know and we'll discuss it. Refer to the paragraph chart for the rules to guide you. Where we decide to indent a paragraph, we will write a backwards "P" with a line through it. That's the symbol editors use to let writers know they need to start a new paragraph. You'll see as we go along.

Here is a sample dialogue for this exercise, which uses the Writing in Paragraphs handout:

TEACHER: *Begins reading text.* When I grow up I want to be a veterinarian. A veterinarian is an animal doctor. I love animals and that is why I want to help take care of them when I am older. I know you have to go to school for a long time to be an animal doctor.

Hmmm. I noticed no one stopped me, so I am going to stop myself. Let's refer to the chart. It says that we begin a new paragraph every time we change the subject or idea. The author begins the text talking about what she wants to be when she gets older. Then she tells you why she wants to be an animal doctor. That sounds like it all fits together. But does the next sentence fit with that first group of sentences? Isn't the next sentence about going to school and how to become a veterinarian? I think it should be a new paragraph, so I am going to put the symbol for paragraph in front of the sentence I want moved. When the student rewrites this draft, the symbol will tell her where to indent. Also, does anyone notice the first sentence of this text? What should the author have done there?

STUDENT A: Indented.

TEACHER: Good! Do you know why?

STUDENT B: Because it is the beginning of her writing and you always indent at the beginning.

TEACHER: Right. Also, it is because it is a paragraph, and you always indent the first sentence of a paragraph. Okay, let's keep going.

Continue reading the text aloud. The students will begin to notice when a new paragraph should start. Their ears will pick it up.

You guys did a good job. Now I'd like you to work with your editing partner and put this excerpt about a girl and her mother into paragraph form. It's labeled Sample 2 on your handout. This text has a lot of dialogue in it. Remember that every time the speaker changes, you need a new paragraph. I don't expect that you will be able to get this right away. Do the best you can, and we'll review it together. I suggest you read it aloud to each other. Hearing it read is a helpful way to pick up when a new paragraph should occur.

Allow students 10 minutes to work on this text. They should stay in the meeting area. Have a whole-class meeting about their findings.

Transition to Independent Work:

Now it is time for you to edit your papers. You will have about 30 minutes to do so. Today, you are looking specifically for paragraphs. To be properly written, your drafts need to be broken up into paragraphs. After you have done this, you may use the Editing Ideas chart to look for other ways to fix the drafts.

Signal the transition to independent work.

This lesson is not only valuable for teaching children how to write in paragraph form, but also for how to work in partnerships. Give them a few minutes to settle in and observe how they work together. Building these working partnerships is key to developing a supportive workshop community. Based on your observations, think of ways you can support partnerships through follow-up mini-lessons.

Confer with Students:

Today you should walk around and look for partners who are having trouble noticing where new paragraphs begin. You may need to pull together groups of children and demonstrate making new paragraphs a second time. You might want to show them a text that they are familiar with from the Reading Workshop and review why the author chose to start new paragraphs in certain places.

Some teachers have even retyped a text students know well without paragraphs. Share such a text, allowing students to see the changes. They will notice something is off and will probably be able to tell you where the paragraphs should go. You can then show them the original text and compare.

Reflect on the Day's Work/Share Our Ideas:

I noticed that some of you were really on task today. I heard a lot of great editing ideas. How many of you were able to recognize where you needed to make paragraphs? What did you change?

A few students should talk about needing to add paragraphs or indent. Here's a example of what that might sound like:

TEACHER: Does anybody want to share the changes they made on their drafts? *Silence.* I noticed that Sam made a really big change in the beginning of his draft. Sam, can you tell everyone what you changed?

SAM: Uh, okay. I was reading my story out loud to my partner and he said I needed a new paragraph, so I made the backward "P" and now it's better.

TEACHER: Good, I'm glad you read your story out loud because that is probably how your partner noticed you needed a new paragraph. But do you know why you needed a new paragraph? What rule did you use to lead you to that conclusion?

SAM: We used the chart and the rule about changing the subject. Because when I read mine I switched from talking about my baby sister to my mom, so my partner said I needed to make that into two paragraphs.

Continue with this conversation as necessary.

Follow-up

- *For homework, students should choose an old entry from their notebooks and edit it for paragraphs.*
- *To reinforce this lesson, you might want to spend one more day going over dialogue in paragraph form, especially because students often publish narratives in this first unit, and they're full of dialogue.*

Final Evaluation: Writing Rubric

By the end of this lesson, students will:

- know how their final publication will be graded;
- know what is expected of them when they present their final project.

Preparation:

1. Supply copies of the Writing Evaluation rubric (see Appendix, p. 155).
2. Create the Expectations for Presentation of Final Draft chart (see below).

Introduce the Lesson:

You should be really proud of yourselves. You are almost finished! Tomorrow you will hand in your final drafts. And then we will have our celebration to mark the end of this Writing Cycle and to honor our hard work.

Teach the Lesson:

Before we begin working on our final drafts, I need to explain the form that your final, published draft must take. Please open your notebook and copy this chart:

The Expectations for Presentation of Final Draft chart reflects the surprises, both good and bad, that we've run into in past years. Make this your own by adding what works for you and deleting what doesn't.

EXPECTATIONS FOR PRESENTATION OF FINAL DRAFT

1. Your final draft is due tomorrow, [date].
2. All late papers will be penalized: 10 points will be taken from the final grade for each day it is late. There are no exceptions.
3. Your final draft should be stapled separately. Your second draft should be stapled separately. Your first draft should be stapled separately. All three drafts should be held together by one large paperclip.
4. You should put the drafts in the following order: Final, second, and first.
   - You should make a cover page that includes the following information: name, date, and class.
   - Your final work should be very, very neat.

Go over your expectations with students. Ask if there are questions. This is the last day they will meet with you before their work is due.

Today you will give your second drafts some last-minute touch-ups. I will hand out an evaluation sheet and you will use it to make necessary changes. This is what we call a "rubric;" it helps the teacher grade students' work. It is a list of the categories of writing elements that I think about when I evaluate your work. It ensures that I am fair, that I assess everyone's work the same way. It is also helpful for you. You can go home tonight feeling confident that you know how your work will be graded.

Hand out the rubrics.

Let's review the rubrics together.

Read the rubric out loud. Spend some time going over each standard. Answer any questions students may have.

Name ______________________

Writing Evaluation

Standard	Above Standard	Meets Standard	Approaching Standard	Below Standard
Student planned the first draft by using an outline or a map in the writer's notebook.				
Student created a first draft by using writing from a variety of entries, not just one.				
Student wrote five different leads before choosing one that catches the reader's attention.				
Student was able to add writing to the draft that was missing and delete writing that did not belong.				
Student work is written in paragraph form.				
Student work has been checked for spelling errors.				

KEY Above standard = 4 points
Meets standard = 3 points
Approaching standard = 2 points
Below standard = 1 point

Transition to Independent Work:

Now that I have shared this evaluation sheet with you, I am sure some of you want to make some changes to your drafts. Use this rubric to help you make the changes. Feel free to work with your editing partner. When you feel confident that you are ready to begin final drafting, you may do so. Whatever you don't finish here, you should complete at home.

Signal the transition to independent work.

Confer with Students:

Today students will really crave your attention. They will ask you to look over their work for final analysis and approval. You should decide how you want to go about this. In our experience, it is easy to become overwhelmed with students seeking your attention on this final day. You may choose not to hold these kinds of evaluating conferences. Let students know that you will be grading tomorrow; today, you want to have conversations about what students think they need to do to accomplish their goals by tomorrow.

Reflect on the Day's Work/Share Our Ideas:

Let's talk about what you accomplished today.

The following is a sample dialogue between teacher and student:

TEACHER: Wilfredo, do you want to tell the class what we talked about in our conference today?

WILFREDO: Well, we talked about the things I need to do to get my final work done.

TEACHER: Like what things?

WILFREDO: I didn't really add much to my draft when we were revising, and I am going to be graded on that, so I started to add writing.

TEACHER: Was that simple, or did you need help?

WILFREDO: You gave me ideas and then Sylvie also helped me figure out where I should add writing.

Remind students of their deadline. Discuss any last-minute questions. You may want to discuss plans for your Writing Celebration (see next lesson).

Follow-up:

- *For homework, students should complete final drafts.*
- *To reinforce this lesson, consider using rubrics whenever you give a grade.*

Publishing: The Writing Celebration

There are many ways to celebrate student writing. Feel free to come up with your own unique way to honor your students' hard work and effort. Here are some of our ideas for celebrating the end of a writing study:

Going Public with Their Work

- Choose three to four students to read their whole drafts aloud. Have them practice beforehand.
- Have all students write a line from their final draft on a sentence strip. Everyone holds up the strip and each student reads a line aloud. Do this as a choral reading.
- Break students into small groups and have them read their papers to one another.
- Display the works on a table and allow students to walk around and read them.

A student reads aloud his first draft.

Making It Special

- Ask students if they want to dress up on the day of the celebration.
- Invite parents, community leaders, neighbors, faculty, and administrators.
- Notify the local newspaper.
- Prepare snacks for after the readings.
- Ask students to respond to one another after a reading by holding an open discussion or writing a quick, positive note to the author.

Whatever way you choose to celebrate, there are some expectations we always share with the class before we begin any celebration. The following is a chart we use when students share their work with the whole class:

DURING THE WRITING CELEBRATION:

- **Keep your draft under your seat while others are reading aloud.**
- **Pay attention to your peers. Make eye contact with them while they read.**
- **Be prepared to write down or share aloud something you enjoyed about your classmates' work.**
- **This is a big deal today. Honor your big day by respecting yourself and those around you.**

The Reading Workshop

Students discuss their books during Reading Workshop.

When we began this work as first-year teachers, we launched Writing Workshop in our classrooms first, becoming comfortable with its structure, predictability, and focused way of teaching. We knew what we wanted our Reading Workshop to look like—kids snuggled in comfortable spaces around our rooms reading books they could read, books they loved even, and sharing this love of reading with each other. If only it could have been that easy! Basically what we were doing was reading aloud to our students, and then having them read silently (or almost silently) as we walked around and tried our best to talk to them about what they were reading. We were nervous being critical about their book choices, nervous about when and how to intervene, nervous about saying anything that might turn them off of reading (even though most of our students already were turned off—in retrospect, it's clear that many of them were just pretending to read for our benefit!). The work that goes into developing and maintaining a Reading Workshop was pretty daunting for us then, mostly because reading happens in kids' heads—how were we supposed to get in there? And what would we find when we did?

In these lessons, we share much of what we learned. Reading aloud and talking with students about the read aloud and their own independent reading is important, but so is clear, direct instruction. Reading Workshop teaching isn't about teaching a book, or a thematic unit. It's about teaching students strategies to support their lives as readers. Reading Workshop teaching necessitates that you reflect on your own reading life: How do you connect with books? How do you choose what you're going to read? How do you deal with difficult text? How do you retell in your mind in order to make sense of reading? As a teacher and a strong reader, you're there to take the mystery out of it all for your students!

In the lessons that follow, we hope to give you a window into that kind of teaching. We believe that in supporting students in becoming stronger readers who engage deeply with text, we can support them in becoming people who engage deeply with the world and the people around them. For we believe that you read in order to learn how to engage with the world, and that reading opens doors that may not have otherwise been accessible.

Introducing the Classroom Library

By the end of this lesson, students will:
- understand genre;
- understand how to use the classroom library.

Preparation:
1. Create the Genre chart (see p. 79).
2. Create the Library Rules chart (see p. 81).

Introduce the Lesson:

This lesson is designed for teachers who have a classroom library—a fairly extensive collection of books inside their classroom. If you do not have a classroom library, you can modify this lesson for the school library. Be sure to include your librarian in the planning! We have found that, with careful planning, the library can become the heart of the classroom.

When setting up your classroom library, ask yourself, Do I have books of different levels and genres? Where should I set up my library? Should the books be in one place or spread around the room? How should my books be organized—by genre? in bins? Are there comfortable places for students to read?

Also consider your lending system: When will students visit the library? How many books may students check out at one time, and for how long? Who monitors book check-out and how? How will students exchange a book they don't like?

Set up your library and your lending system before introducing the lesson today.

If you have a large classroom library and a heterogeneously grouped class, with some struggling readers, you may choose to limit students' book choices this early in the year, sticking to shorter, less complicated texts. We've found that doing this removes the middle-school stigma around "baby books" and makes struggling readers more comfortable in choosing books they can read and comprehend. You can limit your library by putting shorter, lower-level books in baskets from which students will choose or by removing more difficult books from your library for now.

You all know that we're going to be reading and writing a lot in this class. And you may have noticed that we have a classroom library. Our library is full of wonderful books that you can check out and read this year, and today we're going to talk about how the library is arranged and how to check out books to read.

Teach the Lesson:

First of all, I want you to know that you can read books from other libraries and other places. You don't always have to get your reading material from our classroom library. If there's a book you want to read from the school library, or the public library, by all means, check it out and bring it with you for independent reading. We have this library here because it's convenient for all of us. I've put a great deal of thought and time into selecting the books for this library and maintaining it, so I know there are great books in here. Many of them I've read myself, so I can recommend them to you.

Take a look at our classroom library. What do you notice about it? It can be anything—how it's arranged, what kinds of books you notice—anything.

Students might respond: There are lots of books, *or* They're in baskets with the covers facing out, *or* The baskets are labeled with things like realistic fiction, picture books, biography.

Excellent. Let's talk some more about that. You noticed that the books are arranged in baskets and those baskets are labeled. Now there's a fancy word that people use when they're talking about kinds of books. Do you know what I'm talking about? *Silence.* Okay. That's fine. I'll just tell you, and maybe you'll recognize the word. "Genre." Has anybody heard of that word before? *Nodding and hand raising.* I thought so. "Genre" is the fancy word for "kind of book." So look in our library, or think about libraries you've been to before, and think about the different genres of books. We're going to list them on this chart and define them for class reference.

Chart student responses. Your chart might look something like this:

GENRES

Fiction—made-up story, usually a novel or short story

Nonfiction—true story based on real events and facts

Biography—story about the life of a person written by somebody else

Autobiography—story about the life of a person written by that person

Humor—funny story, either true or made up

Mystery—story with a mystery to solve

Poetry—books of poems

Drama—plays, to be performed on stage

Picture Books—fiction or nonfiction books that are illustrated

Realistic Fiction—a made-up story that feels like it could have really happened

Fantasy—a made-up story that could never have happened

How-to Books—books that give you directions for how to do something

Geography/Maps—books of maps

History—books about events and people in the past

Historical Fiction—books that combine real events and people from the past with made-up characters and situations

Have a conversation about genre with your students. It might go something like this:

TEACHER: Okay, so what are some genres you know about or have heard about before?

STUDENT A: Fiction?

TEACHER: Yep. That's a big one. How do you know if something's fiction? What is fiction?

STUDENT B: Fiction is something that's fake. It's like a made-up story that isn't true—the author makes it up.

A classroom library organized with book bins.

TEACHER: Yes. I like that you said, "The author makes it up." So how do you know something's fictional?

STUDENT B: Well, if it's not full of facts and stuff, or if it's a novel. Usually books with characters and stuff are fiction books.

TEACHER: Okay, that makes sense to me. And you're right, a novel is just a fancy way of saying fiction. Also, sometimes you can look on the spine of a book and it'll say "Fic" for fiction. Or, on the inside, near the ISBN number, it sometimes tells you the genre. But let's stick with fiction for a minute because it's a pretty big genre. Are there any other kinds of fiction you've heard about?

STUDENT C: Historical fiction?

TEACHER: Okay, what's that?

STUDENT C: It's got history in it? I'm not sure...

TEACHER: You're on the right track. Let's see if someone can help us out...

STUDENT D: It's fiction, with made up people and stuff, but it's based on real things that happened. Like that book we read last year, *Roll of Thunder, Hear my Cry.* My teacher said that was historical fiction.

TEACHER: Right. And I like that you gave an example. You can see that in our library we have lots of historical fiction books—*Roll of Thunder, Sign of the Beaver, The Witch of Blackbird Pond.* Okay, any other kinds of fiction?

Continue listing genres. Many things are happening in this conversation. Not only is the teacher discussing genre and assessing what her students know, but she is also sharing book titles and talking about what's available for students to read in the library.

Okay, we've got a great list here. Take a minute to look it over and make sure we haven't missed anything. *Give students time to add things or ask questions.* Great. So before I give each table a few baskets of books to look through, I want to quickly go over the rules of the library. Would someone read the first rule?

LIBRARY RULES

1. Library is open for the first 10 minutes of independent work time.
2. Check out 2 books at a time.
3. Keep books for 2 weeks.
4. You are responsible for lost, destroyed, or stolen books. You must replace them.
5. See library monitors to sign out or return books.

Call on a volunteer to read each rule. You might want to explain the rules as you go along.

Today, instead of seeing a library monitor, who will ordinarily be one of you guys, I want you to see me. I'm the temporary library monitor.

Transition to Independent Work:

Now I'm going to put some baskets on each table. Go around and look at the baskets. Become familiar with the contents. If you think that something's in the wrong basket—if it's in the wrong genre—talk about it and bring it up at share time. Look for some books you might want to read, and we'll talk about those during share time too. Also, you might want to think about other kinds of baskets of books we could have here. Maybe there's a genre that's missing. Think about that and we'll talk it over. But most important, get acquainted with the library. You don't have to sign out a book today—we're going to spend more time on choosing books tomorrow. Today I really want you to understand our library. You have about 25 minutes to do this, and then we'll come together to talk about it.

Watch how students interact with books. See who has many ideas for reading and who is struggling just to seem interested.

Confer with Students:

Today you might want to focus on talking to students who are struggling with understanding the library. Talk them through characteristics of major genres. Take them into the library and discuss similarities between the books in one basket. Show them where the genre is listed in the book. Then ask them to tell you the genre of books they've read recently or at least with their class in the previous year.

Poking around in the baskets without looking anything over or saying things like, "I don't like these books" or "These books are boring," are telltale signs of the reluctant and struggling reader. These kids usually haven't had many good reading experiences, so you're going to need to provide those experiences for them this year. Ask them about favorite topics, areas of interest, favorite books that were read to them, books that they wanted to read but couldn't. Steer them to areas of the library where they can find books to hold their interest. Also, keep them in shorter books, so that they can feel success in finishing a book quickly. You also might want to partner them with a student who has read a lot and can introduce them to different titles.

Signal the transition to share time.

Reflect on the Day's Work/Share Our Ideas:

I noticed that people were really getting into looking at the books in the library! Did anyone make some book choices today?

Get student responses.

Are there some changes we need to think about in terms of organizing our library?

Follow-up:

- *For homework, students should reflect on their favorite genres, authors, and books.*
- *To reinforce this lesson, have groups of students take inventory of the baskets, copying the titles of each book onto a small piece of paper and taping it to the outside of the basket. This way, students will be able to easily keep the library organized.*

Guiding Readers Through Book Choice

By the end of this lesson, students will have:

- chosen independent reading books that are appropriate for their reading and interest levels;
- been exposed to nonfiction.

Preparation:

1. Create a blank chart titled Strategies for Making Good Book Choices.
2. Supply markers.
3. Supply book baskets.
4. Supply a varied stack of books for modeling book choice.

Introduce the Lesson:

Today's lesson is about learning to make good book choices. In our own Reading Workshops, we noticed that many of our struggling readers were just grabbing any book off the shelf for independent reading. Our staff developers suggested we model the process of choosing a book for our students. Doing this significantly changed how independent reading looked in our classroom. We began by thinking about how we choose books ourselves. This allowed us to think about how we would model that process for our students.

You know that this year we're all going to read a lot. Every day. I'll read books, stories, and poems aloud to you, but you'll be reading a lot on your own during independent reading time. During this time, you get to read about whatever you want—whatever interests you, in whatever genre you choose, by any author you choose. The only way to become stronger readers is to read, and that's our goal—to become stronger readers, to enjoy what we read, and to learn from it. Because of this, it's important that each one of you is reading a book that is appropriate for you—a "just-right" book. This is a book that is interesting to you, that you want to read, and that you feel comfortable reading—the book isn't confusing or difficult, you understand it. Today we're going to be talking about making those kinds of choices.

Teach the Lesson:

I want us all to think for a minute about how we usually choose a book. What are some of the things that you do?

Students might respond: Read the back, *or* Read the first page, *or* Get a recommendation from a friend.

I'm going to model for you how I choose books—that means I'm going to show you how I'd go about picking a book for myself. Modeling good reading and writing practices is something that I'm going to be doing often. Open your reader's notebooks and get ready to write down what you notice I say and do as I look through this basket of books. I want you to write down what you notice because we're going to talk about it afterwards, and I don't want you to forget any of your ideas.

Use the following example to help you model book choice:

TEACHER: Okay, I've got this pile of books here that I'm going to go through. This book I put in this basket because the cover looked good to me.

Holds up Shark Lady.

I mean, this looks pretty cool—this woman is swimming with a shark! It seems like a nonfiction book, and even though I don't usually prefer nonfiction, last year I had a student, Stephanie, who really taught me a lot about sharks. She read this book and said it was interesting. Now I'm going to look at the back for some more information. Oh, it says here "Scholastic Biography," so I know that it's not really a book about sharks; it's really about this lady, Eugenie Clark. This doesn't really tell me much. I'm going to read the first page.

Open the book and read a little to yourself.

Okay, so this is telling me it really isn't about sharks, but it still seems interesting. I'm going to set it aside because I want to see if there is something that catches my attention more.

Continue modeling this process with other books. You might want to mention pictures in picture books, favorite authors, books people have told you about, award-winning books, books you've read before that you want to reread. After modeling the process with a few other books, stop to ask students what they've noticed.

Okay, what did you notice? What did I do to choose a book?

Chart student responses. After hearing from our students, our charts have looked like the one on the opposite page.

Transition to Independent Work:

Our chart looks great! Good readers use all of these strategies when choosing a book. Now it's your turn. Spend some time looking at the books in the baskets on your tables. You don't have to stick to the basket that is at your table. Use the strategies we talked about today. Think about how you're choosing books. At the share today, we're going to talk about how we made our book choices and what strategies we used. I may confer with you while you are looking for books. I expect to see each of you choosing at least four books from which to make your final selection. If you feel as though you have found good books, start reading them. If you need to sign out a book, see me—the temporary library monitor. And if I could have two volunteers to help, I'll train you to be library monitors.

Choose volunteers who you think can handle the job.

You have about 30 minutes to choose a book. If you choose one before time runs out, find a spot around the room to read it.

STRATEGIES FOR MAKING GOOD BOOK CHOICES

Look at the covers—which ones grab your attention?

Look for titles that interest you.

Pick a book by an author you know and love.

Pick a book in a genre you like.

Read the back of the book.

Read the first two pages to see if it makes sense and grabs your attention.

Read the first two pages to see if the words feel comfortable.

Ask, "Does this seem interesting to me?"

Get a recommendation from a friend.

Look at book reviews.

See if it's won any awards or prizes.

Check if it answers any questions that you have—something you have always wanted to learn more about.

Signal the transition to independent work.

Watch to see if students are using the strategies you modeled. Listen to find out if they are recommending books to each other. If you notice that they are, you might want to ask them to share their recommendation strategy: How do they know what kinds of books to recommend?

Confer with Students:

When you confer with students today, ask them questions about their book choices that help you get to know them as readers but that also support your mini-lesson. Talk especially to students who are struggling with their choice. You might ask: What strategies did you use to find that book? What made you choose that book to read?

If a student grabs just any book off the shelf, stop him right away! Ask what strategies he used to pick it. If he knew that he wanted to read it when we toured the library, ask him why. If he tells you he just grabbed it off the shelf, ask about his reading history to get a sense of his abilities. Take the student through the process of choosing a book. Leave him with a few titles from which to choose (based on his interests) and come back in a few minutes to learn how the final choice was made.

If a student can't (or won't) choose a book, figure out if she has a book in mind that she wants to read but that isn't in your library. You can make arrangements for her to get the book from another classroom or the school library. If someone else borrowed the book the student wanted, try to find something similar. If the student just refuses to choose or read a book (and this doesn't happen very often), it's your job to figure out what's going on. Talk to her about reading, but also do some outside research—call home, talk to her previous teachers (if possible), and find records, such as report cards or reading scores, that might shed some light on why she is so against reading. Also, you need to find out if she can read. You might want to ask her to read a book jacket or chart to you.

Make sure you find one or two students who can talk about their book choice strategies to start off the share time!

Signal the transition to share time.

Reflect on the Day's Work/Share Our Ideas:

I was so impressed by how you were choosing books today! I saw so many of you reading the backs of books and looking for books that have won awards, and I heard people recommending books to each other. These are all habits that good, strong readers have—habits that I want us to build on this year.

When I was conferring today, I asked two people to tell us how they chose their books.

Students share their experiences. Reinforce good habits—not only the strategies you taught but also the practice of listening quietly and respectfully and of speaking loudly and slowly to the group. Share time is when students listen to one another. Make sure they're doing just that!

Students should sign out library books today.

Follow-up:

- *For homework, students should read their books for 20 to 30 minutes.*
- *To reinforce this lesson, show students how and why to abandon books. All too often, struggling readers stick with the same book—one they can't read—because they don't know what reading a "just-right" book feels like, or they don't know they're allowed to exchange books they don't like.*

Keeping Records of Reading

By the end of this lesson, students will have:

- begun a record of books they are reading;
- made plans for their reading.

Preparation:

1. Review and bring in *Thank You, Mr. Falker* by Patricia Polacco (or another book) to read aloud.
2. Supply copies of the Reading Record (see Appendix, p. 156).

Introduce the Lesson:

The other day we talked about making good book choices and the importance of thinking through our choices as readers. Everyone chose a book—and I hope people feel they made the right choices—and we're all reading. We have to read 30 books this year, and it's important that we keep track of what we're reading so that we know how close we are to reaching the goal. Today, I want to show you how we keep records of the books we read.

Teach the Lesson:

I chose the book *Thank You, Mr. Falker* by Patricia Polacco to read to you today. I picked it for a number of reasons. First of all, I've read other books by Patricia Polacco, like *Thunder Cake* and *The Keeping Quilt*, and I've liked them a lot. Also, my friend Jennifer told me this was a good book, and she's usually right about that kind of thing. I read it a few weeks ago, and thought it would be a great thing to read to you. You see, I never just pick up books and read them to people; I always make sure that I think they're good and that someone else would like to hear them. And finally, I thought it was interesting that this book seems like it's fiction, but as you read, you find out that it's really not—it's a memoir. A memoir is a true story from someone's life that has a clear meaning because the writer reflected on it and learned from it.

Before I read it, I'm going to keep a record of it. I'll show you how. I've made photocopies of a kind of record called a "table;" everyone will get a copy. It says Reading Record on the top. I'm going to fill in the title of the book, the author, the genre, and the date I started the book. When I finish it, or if I don't like it and choose to give it up, I'll write the date I finish or abandon it in one of these columns. Each of you is going to get two of these Reading Records to keep in your folders.

The title of our book today is *Thank You, Mr. Falker.* I know that because it says it right here on the cover. The title is usually in the larger type size, or sometimes the title is at the top of the book with the author's name underneath. But that's not always the case. The author is Patricia Polacco. Her name's right here. Sometimes books are by more than one author. In that case, I'd try to write down all of the authors, maybe just their last names, if I could squeeze them in. If I couldn't, I'd just write the first one on the list. Now the genre—we know that it is a memoir. And now the date.

Okay, let's listen and notice how the book tells you it's really a memoir.

You might want to have a brief discussion about students' feelings about the book and their opinions.

What did you notice about how the book tells you it's a memoir?

Students might respond: At the end she says that the little girl is really her, so you know it's a true story.

Good observation! One thing I know is that the more books you read, the easier it gets to figure out the genre of a book. So that's something we'll work on all year.

So now I'm going to record the date that I finished the book here on my reading record sheet. And finally, I'll give it a rating. I have to say, I really like this book. When I read it the first time, it made me cry. For me, any book that can make me cry—that's a 10. So I'm going to give it a 10—the best.

Class ________ Name ________

Reading Record

Title	Author	Genre	Date Begin	Date Abandoned	Date Finished	Ratin (1–10)

Transition to Independent Work:

I'm going to hand out the Reading Record, and right here in the meeting area I want you to write your name on the top and then fill in your independent reading book information—title, genre, author, and the day you started reading it. For most of you, you'll put in yesterday's date.

At this point, there may be some questions about the genre of certain books or even where on the book cover to find the information.

Great. Looks good. Maybe some of you will finish your books today. Does anyone think they will? *Get a show of hands.* Are there some of you who think you picked the wrong book? *Get a show of hands.* If you really think so, you might want to give up on that book—abandon it—and try again. If you need help, I can help you find something you might like better. We have about 30 minutes to read today. Find a place where you can get a lot of reading done.

Signal the transition to independent work.

Take a moment while students are settling in to see if kids are reading. Watch for who starts right away and who has trouble. You might want to meet with kids who are having difficulty getting to work in order to make sure they have the right book.

Confer with Students:

Because today's mini-lesson is about keeping records, you should check to see if students have filled out their forms correctly, especially the information about genre. Talk to students about how they discovered the genre of their book. Ask them to share this with the class.

If a student has filled out the paperwork incorrectly, support her in the area that is giving her trouble. If she is stuck on genre, talk her through the process again. Show her where the genre is listed in the book and what clues the information on the back cover gives about the genre of the book. Have the student correct her form.

Signal the transition to share time.

Reflect on the Day's Work/Share Our Ideas:

It seems that most of us have the hang of keeping records of our reading. I know that finding the genre of your book is the trickiest part. Can we hear from a few people about how they figured out the genre of their book?

Listen to students share their ideas. If this is very difficult for some students in your class, you may choose to chart this information.

Remember, it's important to check the genre of a book and not to rely on where it is in the library, because sometimes books get misplaced and end up in the wrong bins. We're going to keep these forms in our reading folders. Be sure to use them each time you complete a book and every time you start a new one.

Follow-up:

- *For homework, students should read for 20 to 30 minutes independently.*
- *To reinforce this lesson, spend more time having students talk about and recommend books to one another. Also, spend some time reading favorite books aloud, either picture books or the first chapter or so of chapter books to pique student interest.*

Retelling and Reading Comprehension

By the end of this lesson, students will:
- understand why and how readers retell what they've read;
- be able to monitor their own comprehension.

Preparation:
1. Review and bring in *My Grandmother's Hair* by Cynthia Rylant (or another picture book) to read aloud.
2. Create blank charts titled Good Retellings and Why Retell? (see p. 92).

Introduce the Lesson:

The purpose of retelling in conferences is for you to get a sense of your students' understanding of the text. If you've been conferring with your students, you might already have an idea about the problems kids can run into retelling what they've read. We've found that, typically, retellings are either too short without many or any details, or they're too long with tons of extraneous information. Beyond teaching students what a good retelling is, we want to get them to understand that sometimes readers stop and retell something to themselves in order to clarify a difficult part or just to reflect on all that has happened in their reading so far.

Since the very first day, we've been thinking about what it means to be a good reader and to develop the habits of good readers. We're working to make smarter book choices, and we're building our stamina as readers—we're all trying to read for longer, uninterrupted periods of time. Today, we are going to look closely at one strategy good readers use to help them understand what they are reading and read for longer periods of time. It's called "retelling." Most of you have done retellings, or summaries, before. But today I want us to think about two things: what qualities good retellings have, and why readers might want to retell a part of their book.

Teach the Lesson:

While I am reading to you today, I am going to model how to retell parts of a text that may seem cloudy or confusing. Many of you know how to retell—you've all done book reports for which you've had to summarize something. I'm going to model how good readers summarize as they go along to make sure they know what is going on in the story. This can help a reader know if the book he is reading was a wise choice. I'm also going to show you why I choose to retell.

Use the following example to help you model retelling as you read aloud:

TEACHER: This is a beautiful memoir by Cynthia Rylant. It's called *My Grandmother's Hair,* and every time I read it, I notice something new. As I read it aloud to you today, I'm going to model retellings. I want you to listen for two things: what my retellings are like—I mean what qualities they have—and why I choose to retell something. So as I read, I'm going to stop and talk through the thoughts that are going on in my head. Can someone tell me what two things you're going to be listening for?

STUDENT A: We're going to be listening for what your retellings are like—like what they have in common.

TEACHER: Nice. And what else?

STUDENT B: We're listening for the qualities of retellings.

TEACHER: Okay, yes, I think we just said that, but what's the other thing you're listening for?

STUDENT C: Oh! Why you're retelling?

TEACHER: Exactly. What my retellings are like, and why I chose to retell a part of the story. Okay, here we go, *My Grandmother's Hair* by Cynthia Rylant.

Begin reading.

"...Later, I'd watch as she stood before her mirror, taking them out one by one, and her gray locks would be tight as bedsprings and would dance if you pulled on them." Okay, wait, I'm going to stop here because I'm a little confused about this part. I guess I'm not sure what pin curls are. I'm going to think back to what's going on, retell, and see if I can figure it out. Cynthia Rylant, when she was a girl living with her grandparents, loved to comb her grandma's hair. She used a little pink comb on her grandmother's thin hair and they both loved it—it calmed them down, and they would talk about all kinds of things. And then other times they wouldn't talk—they were quiet. And other times she would put bobby pins in her hair to make these things called pin curls and when she took out the pins, they'd be really tight. Oh! I get it. She must take a bobby pin and roll up her grandmother's hair and then pin it to her head with the bobby pin. Then later she takes them out and her grandma's hair is all curly. That part's much more clear to me now. I'm going to keep reading.

Continue to read and retell parts that are confusing or parts that you like and want to think about until you reach the end of the story.

So what did you notice about my retellings?

STUDENT A: You used some details?

TEACHER: Yes, that's true. But did I use all of the details Cynthia Rylant put in her story?

STUDENT B: No, you just picked out some of the more important details.

TEACHER: That's right—the ones that really stuck in my mind. I'm going to write that on our Good Retellings chart. What else?

STUDENT C: You went in order—like, first this happens, then that happens...

TEACHER: Right. Good observation. There's kind of a fancy word for that that reading teachers use. Anyone know what I'm talking about? *Silence.* It's called sequence. I put things in sequence. That means I used the same order Cynthia Rylant did from beginning to end. I'm going to put that on our chart.

Continue adding to the chart until it looks something like this:

GOOD RETELLINGS

- **Are short;**
- **Mention only the important information;**
- **Use the characters' names;**
- **Tell the events in order;**
- **Make sense.**

Now engage students in a conversation about why you retold what you did. It might sound like this:

TEACHER: Excellent. Our chart of the qualities of good retellings looks great. Did anyone notice why I stopped to retell something?

STUDENT A: Well, there was that part about the curls that you didn't get because you weren't sure what pin curls were, so you went back and did a retell and then it made sense.

TEACHER: Right, retelling the story helped me understand this one part that was a little fuzzy to me. Remember how we talked about seeing things in our head like a movie? Well, I couldn't see that part; I wanted to retell it, so it would make more sense to me. So let's put that on the Why Retell? chart. What else?

STUDENT: There was that one part that you liked, so you stopped to think about it, and you did a retelling to remind yourself of the parts you liked.

TEACHER: Good observation. Let's put that on the chart.

Continue charting. When you're finished, your chart might look like this:

WHY RETELL?

- **To clear up a confusing part**
- **To think back, or reflect, on a part you really liked**
- **To figure out what a word means**
- **To get a better understanding of a change in plot**
- **To understand a character better**

Go over both charts quickly with your students. Have student volunteers read off of the list.

Transition to Independent Work:

When you are reading today, stop every once in a while, either during a part that is a little fuzzy that you need to clear up in your head, or just when you think you need to take a break and recap. Then write a brief retelling on a sticky note.

Remember, we keep sticky notes not only to record our thoughts and ideas in this case, the important stuff that's going on in our reading—but also because it really helps me get a picture of what is going on in your head as you read. Also, try to keep focused today—if you need to, look at the chart to remind yourself what you're trying to accomplish.

Once you all get settled in, I'm going to come around and confer with you. Since we're studying retellings, I'll probably ask you to retell for me. You have about 25 minutes to read today. Make them count.

Signal the transition to independent work.

Confer with Students:

As you confer with students, ask them to retell what they've been reading. They could retell what they read last night for homework, if you're conferring when they've just started to read, or what they've just read in class. See what strategies they are and aren't using.

If a student isn't using characters' names, decide if he has a real comprehension problem or just needs to pay attention to who is speaking or acting. Show him how to determine those things. If he says, "This kid is late for football practice," ask, "What kid?" Remind him to get in the habit of using names. Or have the student refer to parts of the book with the characters' names by leafing through the book and pointing them out. He might not be able to pronounce the names, and you'll be able to help him.

If a student tells things out of order, determine, again, if it's a matter of book choice—is she reading a book that is on her level? If she is, you might teach her to use sticky notes to keep track of important plot events. Putting page numbers on the sticky notes and using them for retellings will help students get in the habit of putting things in order in their minds.

If the retelling goes on and on, remind the student that retellings are just the important parts and ask her whether the details she's giving you are really important.

The following is a sample of what this kind of conference might sound like:

TEACHER: We've been talking about retellings today. Can you retell what's going on in your book for me?

Student gives a long retelling with very detailed information.

TEACHER: Okay, hang on a minute. I notice that you're giving me an incredible number of details. Remember, retellings just give the important parts of the story—the key information. What do you think is the key information?

STUDENT: *Shrugs*

TEACHER: Well, take a minute and think through that retelling you just gave me. What's the really important stuff—the stuff you have to know in order to understand the book?

As the student responds, note the differences between her new retelling and her previous one. If the new one works, ask her to continue retelling in this manner. If it doesn't work, teach the student how to discern important information from extraneous details.

Signal transition to share time.

Reflect on the Day's Work/Share Our Ideas:

I noticed that many of you are using our ideas for good retellings, and you're making smart choices about when to retell. Turn to someone near you and retell your reading to that person.

Listen as students retell to each other. Would someone share a brief retelling?

Listen to two retellings or so. Be sure to name for students what they are doing and reinforce good habits. If there's a problem, point it out too. (For example, if a student is struggling to sequence the events in the book as they retell you might say: Thank you! Your retelling was short, you used characters' names, and next time, make sure to tell events in an order that makes sense.)

Why did you choose to retell?

Discussing the process and the value of a strategy helps students understand how to apply it to their own reading. This leads students to become reflective learners.

Follow-up:

- *For homework, students should write a paragraph or two in their reader's notebook, retelling their reading.*
- *To reinforce this lesson, create a mini-lesson in which students use a brief retelling, either verbally or in writing, to recommend their books to another student.*

Building Stamina as Readers

By the end of this lesson, students will:
- have begun to read for sustained periods of time;
- be aware of their distractions as readers.

Preparation:
1. Review and bring in "The First Day of School" from *Hey World, Here I Am!* by Jean Little (or another short story) to read aloud.
2. Create a blank chart titled Keeping Focused as a Reader.

Introduce the Lesson:

For many teachers, giving a lesson on how to read for longer periods of time may seem strange. For us, this lesson came out of necessity. One of the major goals in Reading Workshop is to develop a community of readers who are able to read quietly for sustained periods of time. While for some classes this is a relatively easy task, for others it can be extremely difficult, or next to impossible. Our teaching experience has been with classes full of struggling readers, students who are reading at least two to three grade-levels below where they should be and who have a history of complicated or unhappy experiences with reading.

In our first years of teaching, it was hard to establish a quiet environment where students could read for long periods of time. Working with each other and our staff developers helped us create mini-lessons that both acknowledge our students' problems with reading and teach them to build their own reading stamina. Over time, we saw dramatic improvements in the tone of our classroom and in the amount of reading our students were able to do. This may be a lesson you need to return to—as we do—when you notice students having a hard time sticking with reading.

We're all just beginning our reading lives together in this class, and one of the things we have to do—if we want to meet our goal of 30 books, and if we want to create a strong community of readers—is to be able to read silently for long periods of time. You need to do this for a number of reasons. When you get to high school and college, you're going to be asked to read a lot, and you'll need to read for extended periods of time to get it all done. Also, when you take any kind of test, especially standardized reading tests, you have to sit and read for a while. And I expect you to read a lot in here! Reading for a long stretch of time is something good readers can do. Because we're all working to be good readers, this is something we need to learn. So today we're going to focus on what distracts us and how to avoid those distractions.

Teach the Lesson:

During our read alouds, we're all pretty good—for the most part, everyone pays attention. But I've noticed that we're okay reading independently as a class for maybe 10 or 15 minutes, then people start talking or get distracted and stare off into space, and I have to remind you of what you're supposed to be doing. That doesn't really work for us as a community. First of all, I need to be conferring with individual students during this time; second, I don't want to have to give you frequent reminders; and last, we have to learn to read for longer periods of time to be stronger readers.

So when I read this short piece aloud to you today, not only do I want you to notice your thoughts as readers, but I want you to notice how you keep focused on the read aloud because you're all very good at that.

Begin read aloud, stopping now and then to ask students how they are keeping themselves focused. The reading session might sound like this:

TEACHER: This is a story from a book of short stories by Jean Little called *Hey World, Here I Am!* We have a number of copies of this book in our library, in the "Short Story" basket. I wanted to share this story with you today for a number of reasons, but most of all because I think it addresses some of the emotions we all have in the beginning of the school year.

I'm going to stop in places and ask you to think about how you're keeping yourself focused on the reading, so as you're thinking about the story, think about what's going on in your head to help you pay attention. Okay, here we go:

"Sarah and I think that the first day of school makes you feel like everyone is staring at you all day long. It's like they're looking at what you're wearing, and how you comb your hair, and how much you've changed over the summer."

Okay, I'm going to stop there. Everyone's paying attention—what's going on in your heads?

STUDENT A: I'm remembering how I felt in my new school on the first day, and kind of how I felt here on the first day, and that's helping me to pay attention.

TEACHER: In other words, you're making a personal connection to the story, and that's focusing your attention. Great. Anyone else?

STUDENT B: I'm just thinking about the story.

TEACHER: Yes, I can see that. And you know how I can see that? You're looking right at me. You're seated right in front of me. You've set yourself up from the very beginning to succeed and pay attention. How might that look when you read your own books?

Silence.

TEACHER: Maybe I'm not being clear. If you know that you pay attention better during the read aloud when you're in a place where you're less distracted—right in front of me, where you can see me clearly—how might that look when you're on your own?

STUDENT C: Maybe it's like, you know that if you sit by the window, you're gonna want to look out of it? So don't sit there?

TEACHER: Okay. What do you think?

STUDENT D: Yeah, or if you know that you want to talk to your friend if you sit by them, you decide to sit somewhere else, so that you can keep focused.

TEACHER: These ideas make sense to me. I'm going to write them on our chart right now: "Find a place to read where you're less likely to be distracted—for example, away from windows or friends."

STUDENT A: But what if you like sitting by the window, just for the light, and you don't look out for very long?

TEACHER: Well, I guess that's your decision. I would want to be aware of how much time I was spending looking out the window versus how much time I was spending reading. So maybe I'd look at my watch when I began looking out the window, and then at my watch when I started reading again, to see exactly how much time I was wasting. If I were wasting a lot of time, I'd choose to sit somewhere else.

Continue reading, asking for suggestions, and adding to your chart. When you're finished, your chart might look like this:

KEEPING FOCUSED AS A READER

Make a goal—for example, read one chapter.

Write a sticky note when you feel yourself drifting.

Have a break-book or magazine that you can switch to when you feel you're losing focus.

Use your bookmark to create a goal for your reading.

Try to picture the book in your head like a movie.

Put yourself in the characters' shoes to get lost in the book.

TEACHER: Excellent. Thank you for sharing your ideas. Let's just look back at all of our suggestions. Find one that you think really relates to you—a suggestion that you can use today.

Have student volunteers read them aloud.

Transition to Independent Work:

Turn to someone next to you and tell him or her which suggestion you're going to use today to try to keep yourself focused on your reading. *Listen as students tell each other which suggestion they're going to use. This should only take about one or two minutes.* Can we hear from five people about what suggestion they're going to use and why? *Call on five students to share.* Okay, great.

You have about 20 minutes to read. I'm hoping I won't have to remind you to be quiet after 10 minutes today because you all have ideas about how to help yourselves keep focused. So I'm thinking we'll be able to read for at least 15 minutes in silence, and I'm really hoping we can do the full 20. And don't forget to continue to use your sticky notes.

Signal the transition to independent work.

Take time to watch how students settle in and if they've made different choices about where to sit. You may have to stop students if too many are distracted or talking. Talk to individuals about the suggestion they chose. If you think they made the wrong choice about where to sit, tell them and move them. If the entire class is chatty, you may choose to bring everyone back to the meeting area, refocus them, and send them back to read again.

Confer with Students:

Talk to students about their ability to keep focused. They might not be able to explain to you at first why it is that they were distracted. You will help them learn to do so by engaging them in conversations that require them to be self-aware and reflective.

This conference is your chance to find out what distracts each student. You may want to start by saying, I noticed you were looking out the window. Why? Where did you lose interest in the book? *The book may be too difficult for the student. Check to see if this is the case, and if it is, talk him out of the book and have him choose one that is on his level.*

A student may dislike blocks of description because she doesn't know how to create those images in her head. Teach her how to do this—model it. Then ask her to tell you what she sees when she reads.

If a student really gets into reading, find out what he does and have him tell the class. He's probably reading a "just-right" book, and this is important to acknowledge. He might automatically identify with the main character. The book might answer some questions that he had before reading. He might be picturing the story in his head. Invite this student to share with the class. Hearing about his experiences will be helpful to readers who are easily distracted.

Signal the transition to share time.

Reflect on the Day's Work/Share Our Ideas:

I had some very interesting conferences today. I think we all did pretty well, but reading for a long time takes practice, as you know. You have to work at it. And we're going to keep working. But I'd like to hear from the people I conferred with who were really focused. What were you doing? What happened that allowed you to read so quietly for so long?

Call on the students you conferred with or volunteers who were not distracted during independent reading. You might want to add their ideas to the chart. Our students have suggested tactics like: Get started right away; don't sit near friends; write on sticky notes to keep focused; switch to a magazine if you get bored; make sure you have a book you like.

Follow-up:

- *For homework, students should write a reflection about whether or not they are focused on their reading at home, explaining their answer.*
- *To reinforce this lesson, teach students how and when to change places during independent reading time when distracted or disturbed. If they need a great deal of structure, maybe the spots they choose should become their assigned spots for a while.*

Noticing Our Thoughts As Readers

By the end of this lesson, students will:
- know how to record their thoughts on sticky notes;
- understand that reading is an active process in which their minds are engaged with a text.

Preparation:
1. Review and bring in *Eleven* by Sandra Cisneros (or another text) to read aloud.
2. Have students bring sticky notes.
3. Create the Why Use Sticky Notes While Reading chart (see p. 101).

Introduce the Lesson:

This is the beginning of a series of lessons that reveal the kinds of connections readers make with texts. For this lesson, we want students to know that they are supposed to be thinking as they read. Often, in conferring with students, we've found they don't know that they're supposed to be thinking about what they're reading. Or they're so used to writing a summary book report when they've finished a book that they don't take the time to be aware of their thoughts and ideas as they read. This lesson shows students how and when to take a moment and write their thoughts on a sticky note. This exercise is very important for you as a teacher because the sticky notes provide a window into a student's mind. During a conference, they will help you better understand what is and isn't happening as the student reads.

The other day we learned how to keep records of our reading—a very important thing because we need to keep track of how close we are to meeting our goal of reading 30 books this year. So we've learned a lot about some parts of reading—getting the right book, how the library is organized, how to keep track of what we do, how to stay focused—but we haven't talked about what happens in our heads when we read, and how to keep track of that.

Teach the Lesson:

On your supply list at the beginning of the year I asked you to have sticky notes. I can see that most everyone has some today, and if you don't, I can provide some today—or maybe someone else can give you some—but you have to make sure that you buy your own packet. Remember, these are your tools in this class, and they're your responsibility. We're going to use these sticky notes to keep track of what goes on in our heads as we read.

Let's talk about what goes on in your head when you read. Anything? I mean, besides figuring out what the words are and what they mean—which is a lot of work. But is there anything else?

Here's an example of how this initial conversation might go:

STUDENT A: Well, sometimes I see the story in my head.

TEACHER: Yes, that happens. When you see it, is it like still photographs or is it more like a movie?

STUDENT A: It's more like a movie—things just happening in my head.

TEACHER: Great. That's a sign that you comprehend the book, that you're understanding the words, and turning them into a little movie in your head—something that you can see. Does that happen to anyone else? *Students raise hands.* Good. If it doesn't happen to you, or if you aren't sure, when you're reading today, just take a minute to think about what's going on in your mind, or try to turn the words into images—let yourself see the characters and what they do in your mind. Okay, what else happens?

STUDENT B: I think about what's going to happen next.

TEACHER: Okay. And you're reading a Captain Underpants book, so do you wonder when he's going to turn into Captain Underpants, or if people are going to figure out his real identity?

STUDENT B: Yeah, I wonder what someone might do...

After you hear from a few students, model your own thoughts and how you write those down on sticky notes.

So it seems like we're starting to realize that good readers have thoughts in their heads as they read. The key to becoming better readers—besides just reading a lot—is to become aware of those thoughts. One way to do this is to use sticky notes to record what those thoughts are.

Now, you might be thinking, "Why do I have to write it down? That's going to slow me down when I read!" And you're right, at first it will slow you down a little. But after a while you'll get better at quickly jotting down your thoughts. The reason I'm asking you to do this... well, there are a couple of reasons. First, it makes you aware of what you're thinking, and you can look at your notes and see what you were focused on (maybe a character or an idea) or what your questions were—if the plot was confusing, for instance. Second, when you write those thoughts down, it helps me to teach you better because it lets me see what's going on in your head as you read. When I confer with you, if I can look over your sticky notes and talk to you about them, it's a lot easier for me to see what you're doing as a reader. It's my job to help you become a better reader. Writing your thoughts on sticky notes really helps me do my job. And last, it also helps you talk about your book. You have something you can refer to in a conversation.

It might be helpful to chart the reasons why students are using sticky notes. You can make this chart as you talk through it, or you can make it ahead of time:

WHY USE STICKY NOTES WHILE READING?

- **To help you notice the kinds of thoughts you're having**
- **To help the teacher understand what's going on in your head**
- **To use in a conversation about your book**

I'm going to read another memoir to you. This one's called *Eleven* by Sandra Cisneros. When I read, I'm going to stop in places and show you what I'm going to write on my sticky notes. Notice why I choose to write on a sticky note, where I put it when I'm done, and what I write on the note.

Use the following example to help you model using sticky notes:

TEACHER: *Reads the opening paragraphs and stops.* Okay, I'm thinking something and I'm going to write it down on this sticky note. I'm going to write: "I know how she feels. I'm thirty and some days I still feel like I'm three. I like how she puts it, though—that you're all the ages at once, not just eleven." And I'm going to write the page number on the bottom of the note, so, in case it falls out of the book, I know where it goes.

Teacher keeps reading, then stops again. I just had an interesting thought. I'm going to write it down. I'm going to write, "I like how she makes it really clear—that you're like an onion. I can see the rings and layers. She also could have said it's like a tree trunk, but maybe not everyone knows that trees have rings like onions." And I'm going to put the page number on the sticky note, too.

Keep going—reading, stopping, and writing. Emphasize why you're writing something and that you're including the page number. Keep your writing short. (The reading lesson "Making Connections to Texts" includes a list of ways to respond to texts that might help you plan this lesson.)

TEACHER: So what did you notice? Why did I decide to write on a sticky note?

STUDENT A: When you thought something was interesting.

STUDENT B: When you had a thought, or when you wanted to remember something.

TEACHER: What did I write on them?

STUDENT C: You wrote about how you liked what she was saying.

STUDENT B: And about how people might not know about the rings on a tree.

TEACHER: Yes, very true. But I also wanted you to notice that on every sticky note I wrote the page number. Why did I do that?

STUDENT B: In case it falls out, you know where it goes.

TEACHER: Right.

Transition to Independent Work:

When you go off to read today, I'd like you to use your sticky notes to record your thoughts, as I did. I hope you noticed that when I wrote my notes, I didn't stop after every sentence or anything. Actually, there were more thoughts in my head than I wrote down—I wrote down what I thought was important, something that I wanted to keep a record of. You might use a note for every page, or maybe every few pages. But try to use some today. And don't forget those page numbers! You have about 30 minutes to read today. Make every minute count—get settled and start reading.

Signal the transition to independent work.

Notice how students are getting to work. Give out sticky notes to those students who forgot theirs and remind them to get some.

Confer with Students:

Your goal is to get students to recognize that they have thoughts while they read and to begin getting in the habit of recording these thoughts on sticky notes. If nothing else, students need to know that thinking is part of reading.

Students need practice using sticky notes. If a student isn't doing this, find out why. If he says he has nothing to write, find out if he's thinking as he reads. If he is, ask him why he isn't writing his thoughts down. If he isn't thinking as he reads, find out if the book is too difficult. Using the student's book, model having thoughts about the book. Read parts of the book aloud and ask the student to share his thoughts with you. Then have him write those thoughts on sticky notes.

If, on the other hand, a student is writing far too many sticky notes, talk to her about being more selective. Yes, readers have thoughts all of the time. The purpose of using sticky notes is to provide students and teachers with a window into what's going on. It isn't necessary to write everything down. Students may have a hard time at first being selective. It takes practice.

If a student is writing retellings, ask why. Ask her to think about the other things that are going on in her mind. Is there anything else?

Signal the transition to share time.

Reflect on the Day's Work/Share Our Ideas:

I noticed that people were really getting a good start on using sticky notes. We don't have much time today, so just turn to someone next to you, show them some of the sticky notes you wrote, and talk to them about why you wrote them. *Students should turn and talk while you circulate, listening to what they say. After you think they've said enough—after three or four minutes—ask them to stop talking. Share what you've noticed.* Okay, finish up your conversations…So when I was walking around eavesdropping, I noticed that people were saying they wrote down their most important thoughts or when they thought of something smart that they didn't want to forget. It seems like you're starting to get the hang of this!

Follow-up:

- *For homework, have students read for 20 minutes, look back at their sticky notes, and write a reflection in their reader's notebook about why they wrote the sticky notes they did.*
- *To reinforce this lesson, continue to model why you might stop to write something, and model also that in looking back, you can notice patterns in what you've written.*

Making Connections to Texts

By the end of this lesson, students will:
- see various ways that good readers respond to texts and begin to use some of them.

Preparation:
1. Review and bring in *The Whales* by Cynthia Rylant (or another book) to read aloud.
2. Remind students to bring a supply of sticky notes.
3. Create the How Good Readers Connect with the Text chart (see p. 105).

Introduce the Lesson:

This lesson is a good way to continue the previous one. While that lesson focused on establishing the habit of writing on sticky notes, this lesson gets into the content of those sticky notes, or the specific ways in which readers respond to or think about texts.

When we first talked about how to use sticky notes, we talked about how good readers have many thoughts going on in their heads at once—some of which we might choose to write on sticky notes. Today we're going to talk in greater depth about what some of those thoughts, or connections that we make, might be. You may notice that I'm making some of the same connections you've been making as you read. Today, I want to identify these thoughts for you—to give us a language to use when we talk about what goes on in our heads as we read.

Teach the Lesson:

We've talked about how much work your brain does when you read. And many times, as active readers, we have certain connections with books—thoughts or questions that pop into our heads as we read. You might think about what's going to happen next, or wonder why a character is acting a certain way, or remember when you had an experience similar to an event in your book. Your mind is responding and connecting to the words on the page.

Today, as I read this book aloud, I'm going to model how I respond to a text—I'm going to talk through the thoughts that go on in my head. When you listen, think in two ways—first, pay attention to the story; second and more important, notice the kinds of thoughts I have as I read. Make sure you have your reader's notebooks out and open so that you can take notes on what you notice.

As you read to students, stop in the places where you made a response on a sticky note and share that response with them. You might stop and read sticky notes that say things like, I think this book is more like a poem; I didn't know that mother whales pushed the baby whales up to the surface of the water like that; This drawing reminds me of pictures I saw of my mother's whale-watching trip; I wonder how Cynthia Rylant got so many facts on whales—did she do research? Where is Cape Farewell? I love how Cynthia Rylant uses facts but makes them sound like poetry; This reminds me of a show I saw on PBS about the Great White Whales and how they migrate for long distances; All of the details kind of remind me of something else she wrote, *My Grandmother's Hair. Students should record observations in their reader's notebooks.*

After the read-aloud, engage students in a conversation about what they noticed. It might go something like this:

TEACHER: So what did you notice about how I responded to my reading? What were some of the things I did?

STUDENT A: Well, you asked questions.

TEACHER: Great, can you remember anything I asked?

STUDENT B: You asked where Cape Farewell was.

STUDENT C: You wondered how Cynthia Rylant knew so much about whales, too.

TEACHER: Okay, so I asked a question, and I also wondered about something. I'm going to put those on our chart here...What else?

STUDENT D: You said you liked how Cynthia Rylant made facts sound like poems.

TEACHER: Okay, right. What was I doing when I said that? *Silence.* Let me clarify that—in the other two examples you said I asked a question and that I wondered something. That's what I was doing. When I said I liked something Cynthia Rylant did, what was I doing? *Silence.* I was giving an opinion. When I said I "liked" what she did, I was giving my opinion. I'm going to put that on our chart...What else?

STUDENT E: You said that this book reminded you of the *My Grandmother's Hair* story.

TEACHER: Right. Reading teachers have a fancy way of saying that. We call that a text-to-text connection. One book, or text, reminds you of another text. Text-to-text. I'll write that too. What else?

Continue discussing how you connected with the text until your chart looks something like this:

HOW GOOD READERS CONNECT WITH TEXT

- **Make personal connections**
- **Ask questions**
- **Wonder about things**
- **Notice the author's style**
- **Get inside a character's head**
- **Have opinions**
- **Make predictions**
- **Retell important events**
- **Connect the text to another text**
- **Connect the text to the real world**
- **Have personal thoughts or ideas**
- **Express feelings**
- **Notice important information about the character, plot, or setting**
- **Notice important or interesting facts**

Transition to Independent Work:

Wow! You were very good observers today. You noticed a ton of ways to respond to texts! Turn to someone near you and talk about the kinds of connections you've been making as you read. Also tell them about the kinds of connections you think you'll make when you read today.

Listen as students talk to one another. This should take only one minute or so. You might continue to prepare them for work by having a discussion like the following:

TEACHER: Okay, let's hear from a few people. What are you going to do when you go off to read?

STUDENT A: I'm going to keep making personal connections.

TEACHER: Great. Raise your hand if you think you've been doing that, too...Looks good. Lots of you are noticing you do that when you read. Okay, let's hear from someone else who's trying something different.

STUDENT B: I'm making text-to-world connections.

TEACHER: Wow. That's very ambitious. Anyone else trying that one? Okay, let's hear from one more person...Yes?

STUDENT C: I'm asking questions and wondering.

TEACHER: Excellent—two things: questioning and wondering. Kind of the same, but slightly different, as we noticed. Anyone else doing those? Excellent.

When you go off to read today, think about how you are connecting to texts—be aware of what is going on in your head. Now and then, stop and write a connection on a sticky note. We have about 25 minutes to read quietly. Remember to stay focused.

Signal the transition to independent work.

Watch as students settle in. Move any students who aren't focused.

Confer with Students:

As you confer with students, ask them about the kinds of responses they're having. You might want to ask: What kinds of thoughts are you having as you read? Look at the chart we made: are there any kinds of responses that you always do? Any that you have never done? What happens in your mind as you read?

If a student says nothing goes on in her head when she reads, make sure she's in a "just-right" book. If she is, talk about visualizing the book. This student might need to train herself to see the book as a movie. She could use her sticky notes to record the images she's creating in her mind. That way, you can be sure she's actually doing what you've taught, and you can get a sense of her comprehension based on what the images are.

If a student has difficulty responding to texts, ask him questions to facilitate the process. For example, if the student is thinking about making personal connections but is having difficulty, ask him: Has this ever happened to you? Does this remind you of something or someone from you life? *He could write those questions down to remind himself that those are the kinds of things good readers ask themselves as they read.*

Signal the transition to share time.

Reflect on the Day's Work/Share Our Ideas:

I was really impressed by how quiet and focused everyone was during independent reading time today. I can tell everyone's working on stamina. While I was conferring, I noticed that people were really connecting to their texts. Can we share some of the responses we had to our books and think about what kinds of responses they were?

Hear from a few students.

Follow-up:

- *For homework, students should read for 20 to 30 minutes and write a reflection in their reader's notebooks on the kinds of connections they are making to their texts.*
- *To reinforce this lesson, continue to add new ideas to the How Good Readers Connect with the Text chart.*

Setting Goals for Reading

By the end of this lesson, students will:

- understand the importance of setting goals daily to help them stay on task in Reading Workshop.

Preparation:

1. Review and bring in *Owl Moon* by Jane Yolen (or another book) to read aloud.
2. Supply copies of the Daily Reading Goals table (see Appendix, p. 157).

Introduce the Lesson:

This lesson continues the work from the lesson on building stamina. It allows students to plan for their daily reading. Because this lesson is another way to help students keep on track, use it when you think it will be most helpful. In our experience, students need some way of taking responsibility for their work and need to be held accountable for reading. This lesson is an outgrowth of that need.

We've got a lot going on in our reading workshop right now. Not only are we attending to what goes on in our minds while we read—making connections to texts—but also we've been thinking about how to keep focused, so that we can reach our reading goal of 30 books this year. So we need to think about setting goals for ourselves—making plans for our reading so that we stay on task and also so that we have a direction in our reading.

Teach the Lesson:

So what does it mean to set a goal for reading? Basically, I mean that you think about how much you want to read in a certain amount of time. Figuring out how much you can read in a certain amount of time is part of setting daily goals in reading and keeping focused. But in order to set goals that are realistic—that make sense for you and that are achievable—we need to think about a lot of things. We need to think about ourselves as readers—how fast we read, how much we read, and where and when we try to get our reading done. We need to think about the books we're reading—whether they're challenging, whether we've read them before, how much print is on the page—to see how quickly we can read them and to make sure that we really understand and are getting something out of our reading.

Before I begin our read-aloud today, I'm going to talk you through how I would make a reading goal for myself using our read-aloud text, *Owl Moon* by Jane Yolen. The first thing I'm going to do is figure out how much time I have to read this book. You know how, when we start independent reading, I let you know how much time you have to read? I'm going to think about that for this read-aloud. I usually like to read aloud for 10 minutes or so—sometimes longer, but today I think I just want to keep it to 10 minutes so we have a lot of time to read independently. So I'm going to make a plan for this read-aloud.

Hand out copies of the Daily Reading Goals table. Talk your students through filling it out. Use the following language to help you begin a conversation about setting goals:

Daily Reading Goals

Title	Date	Goal	Time Start	Page Start	Time End	Page End	Goal Reached

TEACHER: Okay, so the title is *Owl Moon,* and today's date is October 25th. Now, let's see...what is my goal going to be? For that, I really need to look over this book. It's a picture book, so they're usually shorter. Most of the time, I can finish reading you a picture book during the read-aloud. But sometimes, picture books can have a lot of text in them. I remember Cynthia Rylant's book *Appalachia* looks like a skinny picture book, but there are lots of words on the page. So I'm going to look and see if this seems long or short. Let's check it out.

Teacher opens the book, turns the pages, and shows the text to the students.

TEACHER: What do you think? Some of the pages have small amounts of text on them, but others...looks like kind of longish paragraphs to me. What do you think? Does this look like a 10-minute read?

STUDENT A: I think you could read it in 10 minutes.

TEACHER: Why?

STUDENT A: Well, I think that if you read all the way through, like if you just keep reading, it'll be okay because you're kind of a fast reader.

TEACHER: Oh, I see. Do you mean you think I'll be able to read it faster because I probably know all of the words and I won't stumble over them when I read out loud?

STUDENT A: Yeah.

TEACHER: Okay. That makes a lot of sense to me. But think about what happens when we read aloud. Do I always just read right through? What do we do? What happens?

STUDENT B: We stop and talk about what we think. Or sometimes you stop and tell us what you think, like, what you wrote on a sticky note?

TEACHER: Uh-huh. Just as when you read, you stop every once in a while and write something on a sticky note, I stop and take some time to tell you what I'm thinking—what I wrote on my sticky note or the kinds of connections I'm making to the text. Right. So that takes up some time too. So I think if we read for 10 minutes, and we stop every so often and I talk about my thoughts, and then we stop and you turn to someone and talk about your thoughts...I don't think we'll finish the book. But I think we'll get very close. Maybe we'll have five pages of text left or something like that. So I'm going to write that as my goal. This book doesn't have page numbers, so it's tricky to write a goal. I'll say, "Stop five pages from the end in 10 minutes." Okay. We're starting at 9:20, so I'm going to write that on our goals sheet, and we're starting on page one so, I'm going to write that too. So let's read it and see how we do.

Read text. Stop in places and model your thoughts as a reader—make connections. You might say: I'm not sure what "owling" is. I've never been owling, but I can infer that because they're walking in the woods at night, it must just mean that they're looking for owls. I know that owls are only out at night—they're nocturnal animals. *Or,* I love the descriptive language Jane Yolen writes. I can really hear the snow crunching under her feet.

Try to meet your goal of almost finishing in 10 minutes. At that point, because you're so close to the end, you might choose to continue a few more minutes and complete the book. If you manage to finish it in 10 minutes, be sure to make note of that. Remember that the point is to get used to making and meeting daily goals. This is what it might sound like to discuss these goals with your students:

TEACHER: Okay. So we finished the book, and it did take us a little longer than 10 minutes. But we met our goal. Actually, we did more than meet our goal. We exceeded our goal. Do you know what I mean by that? To exceed our goal?

Silence.

TEACHER: Well, let's think about it for a minute. If our goal was to reach four or five pages before the end in 10 minutes, and we finished the book in 11 minutes and I'm saying we exceeded our goal...What do you think exceeded means?

STUDENT A: To do better than your goal?

TEACHER: Kind of, yes. To go past your goal. If you exceed something you go beyond it. We went beyond our goal because we finished the book. So let's finish filling out our daily goals sheet. We wrote that we read *Owl Moon,* today's date, that our goal was to get very close to the end—four or five pages away—and that we started at 9:20 on page 1. We ended at 9:31, on the last page, so I'm going to write that. Now it says, "Goal reached." That's where you write either "yes" or "no," or "I came very close," or, as we did, "I exceeded my goal," meaning I read more than I thought I would. So I'm going to write that: "I exceeded my goal."

Pass out the Daily Reading Goals sheet for students to keep in their reading folders. At the meeting area, have students fill in the title of their book, the date, and their reading-time goal (probably around 30 minutes).

Transition to Independent Work:

Right here at the meeting area, make a goal for yourself for reading. Keep in mind that you're going to be reading for 30 minutes as well as stopping to write sticky notes every once in a while. Fill out the title, date, page-start, and goal. Take a minute to do that now.

Watch to make sure that students are filling out the sheet correctly and making reasonable goals for themselves.

Can we hear from four people about what their goals are in reading today?

Listen to students.

You're going to have about 30 minutes to read. You should get started right away in order to meet your goals. Don't forget to record the connections you make to your book on sticky notes, and don't forget to write the page numbers on the notes. If you don't have any sticky notes, you can use your reader's notebooks to write your connections. If you reach your goal before 30 minutes is up, keep going. You'll exceed your goal!

Signal the transition to independent work.

See who gets started right away and who has trouble getting it together. Watch to see if students who had problems before get to work faster now that they have made a goal for themselves. You might want to confer with students who are still struggling to read—perhaps they have chosen inappropriate texts.

Confer with Students:

In your conferences, ask: What is your reading goal? How did you decide that should be your goal? How are you working to meet your reading goal today? How did having a goal change the way you started reading today? How is having a goal keeping you focused? What are you doing to meet your reading goal? Do you think your goal is realistic or unrealistic? Why?

If a student isn't making realistic goals, have her use today's reading time to test how much she can read in 30 minutes. She can use this information to help her set goals in the future.

If a student is making bad choices about where to sit, set some ground rules about places he can't sit or people he can't sit near. Maybe he needs an assigned spot for reading until he can learn how to work independently.

If a student is reading a great deal and getting started right away, talk to the student about how she does this. Ask her to share her ideas about how she stays focused.

Signal the transition to share time.

Reflect on the Day's Work/Share Our Ideas:

Focus on the process of meeting goals.

Take a minute and on your goal sheets, fill in the Time End and Page End, and then write "yes" or "no" in the Goal Reached column. *Give students a minute. You might need to remind them of the time they stopped reading.*

I noticed that having a goal really helped a lot of you get started right away and stay focused. For those of you who are still struggling with that, maybe it's time to take an honest look at your book and ask yourself if it is "just right" for you. Okay, raise your hand if you reached your goal today. *Wait for students to raise their hands.* Raise your hands if you didn't meet your goal today. *Wait for students to raise their hands.* Okay, those of you who met your goals, what do you think you did that made that possible? What choices did you make that worked for you? *Listen to students. If necessary, add responses to the Keeping Focused as a Reader chart.* Those of you who had trouble meeting your goal today, can you talk a little bit about what happened and what you might do differently?

Listen to students. Encourage them to learn from this.

Remember, this is the first time we're doing this, and sometimes it takes a while to learn to make realistic goals for ourselves. The point is that we're working on building our stamina—our ability to sit and read for extended periods of time.

Follow-up:

- *For homework, students should set a goal for their reading at home. To involve parents, have them initial the goal sheet for that night.*
- *To extend this lesson, show students how to set larger reading goals for themselves—to keep lists of books they want to read next, to plan their own author studies, to work on reading a new genre. Students can also keep back-up reading material with them for when they're losing interest in their main book. (Back-ups might include picture books, short stories, or magazines.)*

Making Personal Connections When Reading

By the end of this lesson, students will:
- know that good readers make personal connections with texts;
- know ways to make personal connections with the texts they read;
- understand that making personal connections with a text does not always mean having had the same experience as one of the characters.

Preparation:
1. Review and bring in "My Best Friend" by Eloise Greenfield (or another book) to read aloud.
2. Create a blank chart titled Personal Connections (see p. 115).

Introduce the Lesson:

Today's lesson is a more focused version of the "Making Connections to Texts" lesson. It takes one of the ways that you can make connections to a text—personal connections (or text-to-self connections)—and breaks it open, making it more explicit. Modeling this for students clarifies what it means to connect to a book. Also, it demonstrates to students that not all personal connections to readings are of the "This reminds me of…" kind.

The other day we talked about how good readers respond to texts and listed the different kinds of connections you can make as you read. *Refer to the How Good Readers Connect with the Text chart that should be hanging in your classroom.* We noticed that sometimes readers make personal connections as they read. Today we're going to focus on those personal connections—what they are and some of the many different ways readers can make personal connections to a book. *You might want to circle the personal connections item on the list, or put a star next to it.*

Teach the Lesson:

Take a minute and look at some of the sticky notes in your independent reading book. Find one or two that you think are personal connections. If you've been using your reader's notebooks for connections, look there. I'll give you about two minutes to do this. *Wait until students have found at least one personal connection.* Okay, turn to someone near you and share your personal connections. *Listen to the kinds of connections they are making.* Okay, can we hear from three or four people? What do your personal connections sound like?

Students might respond: This reminds me of when I had a fight with my sister; *or* I remember my first day of school.

That's excellent. You are getting the hang of one kind of personal connection—when you read something that reminds you of something you have experienced. I'm going to write that on our chart. "This reminds me of..." But I also want you to see that there are other ways of making personal connections.

I'm going to read a story by Eloise Greenfield called "My Best Friend." As I read, I'm going to be modeling how to make personal connections. I want you to listen for the different kinds of personal connections I make. You can use your reader's notebooks to take notes.

As you read, stop and make personal connections. Try to make different kinds. Here are some examples: My best friend growing up didn't live near me, but when we were together in school we would talk and talk! *or* I never did anything like this with my best friend, but I can relate to the important stuff—that they were just together, talking; *or* I felt the exact opposite about the piano—I played it, but I didn't like it very much! *or* I never did anything like she did—build a whole city; *or* I can't really relate to this—I wasn't much of a planner as a student; *or* I don't think I ever made detailed plans about my future—I had just little ideas.

After the read-aloud, ask students what they noticed and if they made any personal connections they want to share. The conversation might sound like this:

TEACHER: Okay, what did you notice? What kinds of personal connections did I make—or what did they sound like?

STUDENT A: You said how you didn't live near your best friend?

TEACHER: Right, I was saying that what I was reading wasn't true for me, it didn't happen, but that I could still relate to it. Let's put that on our chart like this: "That didn't happen to me, but..." What else?

STUDENT B: You said that you couldn't relate to the character?

TEACHER: Yes. What does that mean, when you say you can't relate to something?

STUDENT C: That it never happened to you.

TEACHER: Yes, but sometimes it's a little more than that. Can someone help?

STUDENT D: Like, it didn't happen to you and so you don't really understand it all that well—like, it isn't your experience?

TEACHER: Yeah, exactly. So let's put that on our chart: "I can't relate to this..." You can say that you can't relate to a character or to something that your character does. You can even say that you can't relate to a whole book because what happens in it is so far from your own experience. But just because you don't relate to something doesn't mean you can't appreciate it or learn from it.

When you finish, your chart might look like this:

PERSONAL CONNECTIONS

"This reminds me of..."

"I remember..."

"I've seen this before..."

"That happened to someone I know..."

"That happened to me..."

"That never happened to me..."

"I can relate to that because..."

"I can't relate to that because..."

Transition to Independent Work:

You're going to have about 20 minutes to read today. Right here in the meeting area, take out your reading goals sheet and make a goal for yourself. You have two minutes. *Give students time to make their goals.* Okay, let's hear from a few people. What are your goals? *Hear from three or four volunteers.* What are you going to do to keep focused and reach your goal? *Listen to three or four students.*

Today when you read on your own, focus on making personal connections where it's possible. Think about different ways that you can make personal connections. Remember, the book doesn't have to describe your exact experience for you to connect to it. You have 20 minutes.

Signal the transition to independent work.

Confer with Students:

Learn how students are making personal connections. You might ask: Can you tell me about some of your personal connections? Describe a personal connection you made to what you read last night—how are the connections you're making today different? What kinds of personal connections are you making today? Is there a kind of personal connection you're using a lot? Why?

If a student isn't making personal connections, first make sure her book is on an appropriate reading level. Then make sure it is in a genre that makes sense for personal connections. Ask to see the student's sticky notes from previous days. Maybe she made other kinds of connections, just not personal ones, which is fine. If she isn't connecting at all, ask questions to get her to start thinking about herself in relation to the book.

If the student is reading nonfiction, first ask to see the kinds of thoughts he's been recording on his sticky notes. If he's doing well and seems to be engaged and thinking about the text, you might have him continue his work. Or you could give him ways to personally connect to factual texts—plan ways to use the facts he's learning, see how the facts relate to his day-to-day life, and so on.

Signal the transition to share time.

Reflect on the Day's Work/Share Our Ideas:

Take a minute and fill in where you stopped reading and if you met your goal. *Give students a minute.* How many people met their goals? *Wait for hands.* Exceeded? *Wait for hands.* Didn't meet? *Wait for hands.*

How'd that go today? Were people making different kinds of connections? How many people felt that they tried a new way of connecting to a text today? *Wait for a show of hands.* Excellent. Turn to someone near you and share a new way of making a personal connection that you tried today. *Listen to students as they discuss their ideas.* Can we hear from two or three people? *Listen to responses, adding to the Personal Connections chart if appropriate.*

In my conferences, I noticed that people were talking a lot about how they were different from the characters rather than just how they were like the characters. That's an interesting way of connecting. To take it further, you might want to think about what you're learning from that character because he or she is different.

Follow-up:

- *For homework, students should continue to write about personal connections in their reading notebooks.*
- *To reinforce this lesson, continue to add to the list of ways to make personal connections. Have students teach the mini-lesson by sharing their sticky notes.*

Asking Questions as We Read

By the end of this lesson, students will:
- know how to ask themselves questions as they read to monitor their understanding;
- know how to ask questions to deepen their comprehension;
- have gained insight into the nature of nonfiction.

Preparation:
1. Review and bring in *Chomp* by Melvin Berger (or another book that is a relatively easy text) to read aloud.
2. Create a blank chart titled Readers Ask Questions To (see p. 119).

Introduce the Lesson:

We've been talking about the different ways that good readers respond to texts. We've talked about different kinds of connections they can make, and we've looked more closely at making personal connections. Today I want to talk about another way that readers respond to texts—by asking questions.

Teach the Lesson:

Readers ask questions for many different reasons. A reader might ask a question to try to understand why a character is doing something or acting in a certain way. A reader might ask a question to clarify something that's happening in the plot or to better understand a fact or idea.

Today I'm going to model for you the kinds of questions a reader might have while reading a nonfiction book. If you're reading fiction, the kinds of questions you ask will be different. We'll talk about those after the read-aloud. As I read today, notice the kinds of questions that I ask.

While read-alouds are typically either short picture books or texts on a higher reading level, today's read-aloud is a lower-level text. We chose this one with struggling readers in mind. Reading it aloud promotes lower-level books in your classroom and serves to remove some of the stigma around choosing "easy" or "baby" books. Also, reading the first few pages can pique the interest of readers on several levels, and they might want to check it out from the library when you're finished!

When you're planning for the read-aloud, think about the kinds of questions you want your students to ask. If you have noticed that they aren't good at monitoring for understanding, ask questions that demonstrate how they can help themselves make sense of a confusing part. You might say: Wait a second, I don't get this part. I wonder if... *If your students don't know how to ask questions that lead them to making predictions about texts, model those for students. Say, for example:* I wonder if x is going to happen next because it said that...

Use this example to help you model asking comprehension questions:

A teacher leads a class discussion.

TEACHER: What kinds of questions did you notice I was asking?

STUDENT A: You asked what kinds of food sharks eat.

TEACHER: Okay, so how can we write that on our chart? What was I trying to do?

STUDENT B: You were wondering something?

TEACHER: Okay, let's put that on our chart. What else?

STUDENT C: You asked what happened to the seal.

TEACHER: Right. How can we say that?

STUDENT C: You could say that you were trying to understand what happened?

TEACHER: Sounds good. What else?

STUDENT D: There was that part where you asked why, if the shark has so many teeth, it swallows the chunk of the seal's flesh whole.

TEACHER: Right. That's a complicated question. How can we say that?

Silence.

TEACHER: Well, tell me if this makes sense. I was trying to understand the facts they were giving me in the book. What do you think? Can we chart it like that? Okay. What else?

Continue charting what students notice (see the Readers Ask Questions To chart, opposite, for some things you can expect students to say based on your modeling).

At some point, you will need to discuss the sorts of questions a reader can ask about fiction. Use this language to help you model asking comprehension questions about a fictional text:

TEACHER: What kinds of questions do you think come up when you're reading a fictional text? Those of you who are reading fiction, take a minute to look at your sticky notes. See if you've written any questions and think of how we might write about them on our chart. *Give students time to think.* Turn to someone and share what you're thinking. *Give students about two minutes to talk about it.*

What do you think? What kinds of questions can you ask about fiction?

STUDENT A: Well, in my book I asked where they were. I wasn't sure where they were, and so I asked where are they?

TEACHER: Does anyone know what the fancy word for that is in a book—where they are? Where the book takes place?

STUDENT B: The setting!

TEACHER: Right. So you could ask a question about the setting. Let's add that to our chart. What else?

STUDENT C: You could wonder why something is happening. In my book, I wondered if Lena was going to find her mom or not. It's like wondering what was going to happen next—if they were going to get to do what they wanted to do.

TEACHER: Interesting. Okay, so you were asking a question about what was going to happen next. Let's chart that.

Continue taking student responses. If they have trouble making this leap to fiction, you may have to do a read-aloud demonstrating questions in fiction in a follow-up mini-lesson. For now, add strategies to the list and explain them briefly, if kids have difficulty offering up suggestions. This way, those students reading fiction will have something to work on during independent work today. At the end of the class discussion, your chart might look like this:

READERS ASK QUESTIONS TO

- State our wonderings
- Understand something that happens in the book
- Make sense of facts
- Clear up confusing parts
- Determine the setting of the book
- Figure out what's going to happen next
- Understand the characters and why they do what they do
- Understand why the author writes like she does
- Voice an opinion
- Figure out the plot

You may want to divide this chart into Fiction and Nonfiction questions (a T chart) if you feel your students need that distinction made clear for them.

Transition to Independent Work:

Looks good! Today when you go off to read, remember how good readers ask questions. You might want to make sticky notes for things you wonder about, questions that you have about facts, or about the plot, or something that doesn't make sense to you. Take a minute now to look at the chart to remind you of the different kinds of questions readers think about. *Give students about a minute.* So what do you think? Who thinks they might focus on questions as they read today? Any particular kind? *Take student responses, being sure to ask why they're choosing to focus on a particular question because you may need to steer them in a direction that is genre-appropriate. If a student is reading fiction, for instance, and chooses to "make sense of facts," his time may be better spent "clearing up confusing parts" or "understanding the characters."*

You have about 30 minutes to read today. Before we go off, take out your goal sheets and make a goal for yourself. You have two minutes to make a goal. *Give students time to write goals, supporting struggling students.* Can we hear from three people? What are your goals? *Listen to goals, making suggestions when necessary.* Remember, we're reading for the whole time, so if you meet your goal, keep reading; you will have exceeded your goal for today. I'm going to come around and confer with you about your questions, and we'll share our ideas after we read.

Signal the transition to independent work.

Confer with Students:

Talk to students about the kinds of questions they are asking in their heads. If a student is asking questions that indicate that she does not understand her book, be sure to direct her to another book. Also, let her know that when she finds herself not understanding parts, she should go back and reread.

When conferring, you might ask: What kinds of questions do you think you're asking? What made you ask that question? How do you think these questions are helping you to understand the book?

If a student is asking a lot of questions to clear up confusing parts, first make sure the book isn't too hard for him. Then teach the student to reread the confusing parts. Talk about where it is that he loses his sense of the story. Does he need to go back even farther in the book?

If a student is asking questions about the meanings of words, make sure this isn't happening so often as to cause major problems with comprehension. Then teach the student strategies for dealing with those words, like learning prefixes and suffixes; breaking the word into chunks (finding words within words, like under *in* undergarment *or* bed *and* post *in* bedpost*); looking for context clues; picturing the situation to ready her mind for what words might be on the page; and seeing patterns in words (groups of letters that are familiar from words the student knows, as in* right, tight, light, *and* sight*).*

If a student is asking many questions, you might want to teach him to remember some of the questions in order to find answers for them in the text.

Signal the transition to share time.

Reflect on the Day's Work/Share Our Ideas:

Before we start the share I want you to take a minute and fill out your goal sheets. *Give students a minute.* Show of hands—people who exceeded their goals? *Wait for hands.* You might think about making harder goals tomorrow. People who met their goals? *Wait for hands.* Nice work. People who didn't meet their goals? *Wait for hands.* You need to do some thinking about why you didn't meet your goal today. I've got some ideas, and I can speak with you individually later on.

Okay, on to the share. As I was going around and conferring with all of you, I was amazed by how many questions you were asking! What was it that made you ask questions? What kinds of questions were you asking? *Listen to the ideas of a few students. Add to the Readers Ask Questions To chart, if appropriate.*

I just want to remind people that if you notice that you are asking a lot of questions to try to make sense of something—if you just don't get something in your book—go back and reread the confusing part. If that doesn't help, you might want to think about whether or not you've chosen a book that's right for you. Remember, struggling with a book that isn't right for you isn't the way to become a stronger reader. You'll just get bored, frustrated, and not want to read.

Follow-up:

- *For homework, students should continue to ask questions about their books. You might ask them to do this in their reader's notebooks. They might choose to focus on a particular type of question.*
- *To reinforce this lesson, model asking questions about a piece of fiction. Add those ideas to your chart.*

Making Predictions as We Read

By the end of this lesson, students will:
- have used predictions to support their comprehension of a text;
- know how to support predictions with evidence from the text.

Preparation:
1. Review and bring in *I Hadn't Meant to Tell You This* by Jacqueline Woodson (or another book to read aloud).
2. Create the chart titled Questions to Ask when Making Predictions (see p. 123).

Introduce the Lesson:

In our experience, students love to make predictions. They are used to making predictions while watching TV and movies, but they might not know how to do it when reading.

A number of things can stand in the way of students making good predictions. They might have limited exposure to a certain genre, or they might have limited exposure to reading in general. For these readers, model how your understanding of a genre helps you predict accurately. You might say, This book sounds like realistic fiction to me, so I imagine that what goes on in this book will feel like real life, *and then go on to make your prediction. Because of their limited experiences with reading and their subsequent lack of exposure to a variety of genres, these students need to read more and to be coached to make connections between the books they read.*

Also, some students aren't used to finding clues or evidence to support their predictions. Modeling how to use evidence—and where it came from—is especially important for them.

For the past few days, we've been looking more closely at ways readers can respond to texts. We've looked at personal connections and asked comprehension questions. Today we're going to talk about making predictions and how it can help you to understand your book. Also, we're going to talk about the importance of finding evidence to support your predictions.

Teach the Lesson:

What is a prediction? Does anyone know? *Take student responses briefly. If they don't know, just tell them. You might say, "A prediction is a guess about what's going to happen next." You might link predicting to science by talking about hypothesis—an educated guess about the outcome of an experiment.* So we're interested in predicting what's going to happen in our books. But how do you come up with a prediction? What causes you to make a prediction? *Take student responses. Students might say, "Books give clues, or It's just a feeling you get from reading."*

Today I'm going to model how I make predictions. As I read aloud, I'm going to stop and make predictions. I'm also going to talk through why I'm making certain kinds of predictions about my book or where I'm getting the evidence to support my ideas. What do you think that means, "evidence to support my ideas"? *Take student responses. Lead students to say something like,* Finding details in the book that show your prediction makes sense. *If they can't get there on their own, tell them.*

I've prepared a chart of some of the things I think about when I'm making a prediction. Let's take a minute to read through it.

Read the Questions to Ask when Making Predictions chart aloud (or have students volunteer to read it) and give explanations when necessary. The purpose of this chart is to get kids to think about the things that trigger predictions in readers, as well as the kinds of questions readers ask to make sure they're making their best predictions.

QUESTIONS TO ASK WHEN MAKING PREDICTIONS

- **What do I know about this genre?**
- **What makes sense for this character—based on what I know, would the character do or think something like this?**
- **Would my prediction make sense with the plot?**
- **Is it something the author would do—based on what I know about the writer, is it something that he or she would put in a book?**
- **Do I have evidence (proof from the book) to support my prediction?**
- **Is there any other information that gives clues about the story—pictures, the cover, the information on the back?**

When I make predictions today, I'm going to use this chart to help me. Try to notice where my predictions come from—what I'm thinking about as I make them. You might also like to make some predictions of your own as I read.

Use the following example to help you model making predictions:

TEACHER: Even before I start reading, just by looking at the cover of this book, I can make a couple of predictions. First of all, it's by Jacqueline Woodson. I've read some of her books before and they're usually realistic fiction—a story that's made up but sounds real. So it will probably take place in a realistic setting and be about people who seem real, who are going through things that people really experience. I also know that she likes to write about certain themes, and the cover gives me clues about that too. Woodson likes to write about race. And I notice that there's a black girl and a white girl on the cover, so I predict this book might be about a black girl and a white girl being friends and what that means in terms of confronting racism. Also, this book's won an award—a Coretta Scott King award. I know that Coretta Scott King is Martin Luther King Jr.'s wife and that her awards are given to books that honor Martin Luther King's memory—books about overcoming prejudice and developing racial understanding. So I predict it's going to be a book about that.

After reading the back, I can see that my prediction from the cover seems right, but that there's a lot more to this book. This secret seems scary. If Lena wants to protect herself from her father, I wonder if he's abusive?

After reading the poem by Emily Dickinson that opens the book, I think it's going to be a sad book. The word "agony" makes me think that. "Agony" means terrible, terrible pain. So I predict that maybe one of the characters in the book is in great pain.

Just hearing about the town of Chauncey— the changes the town went through, blacks moving in and problems with the poor whites—I predict that there will be real racial tensions there.

Keep making predictions and showing evidence for your ideas.

What do you think? What do you think I was thinking about as I made my predictions? Look at the chart. Did I do any of those things? *Call on students and support them in pointing out the strategies you used to make predictions.*

Did anyone make predictions that I didn't think of? *Call on a few students. Be sure to ask them why they are making their predictions—what evidence they have for their ideas. Chart their ideas, if appropriate.*

Transition to Independent Work:

The thing I really want you to think about today is making sure that your predictions make sense. I'm leaving the chart here, so that if you need to ask yourself some questions to help you make a prediction, you can do that as you read independently.

Before we go off to read, set a goal for how much reading you're going to do today. We're going to read for 30 to 35 minutes. Once you've made your goal, turn and share it with someone near you. You have two minutes to do this. *Make sure students have written a goal and shared it with someone.*

Okay, as you're reading your books today, if you're in a genre that allows you to do this, stop every once and a while and make predictions. *Some genres are more difficult to make predictions about, like poetry and fact-heavy nonfiction, so you might want to take students who are reading those genres aside and suggest they continue with another strategy, holding off on making predictions for the time being.* I'm going to be coming around to confer with you and see how it's going, so be prepared to talk to me about your predictions.

Signal the transition to independent work.

Confer with Students:

Notice how students are making predictions as you confer with them. If you notice that many are having difficulty or aren't using evidence, then you should continue with this work in the next few days.

If a student is making predictions that don't make sense, first make sure she comprehends the book. When pre-

dictions seem like they come out of nowhere, the student may be trying to mask her lack of understanding. If this isn't the problem, ask her where in the text her idea is coming from. Sometimes students don't refer back to the text to support their predictions, and they need to learn how to do this.

If a student is making predictions that make sense, ask him to show you the evidence for these predictions. If he can do this, you might want to teach him to check if his predictions are correct or will need to be changed. To go even further, in a subsequent conference you might want to teach him to focus his predictions (at least the ones he keeps track of on sticky notes) on a certain character. If his predictions are incorrect because the character changes over time, he will be able to track where and why the character changes.

A conference might sound like this:

TEACHER: Have you made any predictions in your reading today?

STUDENT: Yeah.

TEACHER: Can you talk to me about them? Show me a sticky note that records a prediction.

STUDENT: Well, here on page 18 I wrote, "I think Melanin is going to have a problem meeting his mother's date."

TEACHER: Why did you write that?

STUDENT: Well, um, I was thinking about Melanin's attitude.

TEACHER: Okay, what about his attitude? Is there something in the book?

STUDENT: Yeah. On the page before he's talking like he really doesn't want to meet his mom's date. He's complaining about having to go to dinner. See? So I think he won't like this guy his mom's bringing home.

TEACHER: Oh, I see. So you asked yourself the second question: What makes sense for this character?

STUDENT: Yep.

TEACHER: Have you learned anything else about Melanin that makes you say this?

STUDENT: *Silence.*

TEACHER: It seems to me you're thinking about his character traits—different parts of his personality that make him act the way he does. You might want to keep track of these character traits on sticky notes as a way to see if your predictions about the way he acts make sense.

STUDENT: *Nods.*

TEACHER: So I'd like you to try that—to keep track of his character traits as a way to check your predictions. Okay, just so we're clear, what is it that I want you to try?

STUDENT: You want me to write the character traits of Melanin on a sticky note.

TEACHER: And why are you doing this?

STUDENT: To keep track of whether my predictions make sense—to gather evidence.

TEACHER: Very good. And just tell me what we mean by "character traits," so I know we're clear?

STUDENT: The way he acts and thinks, like the parts of his personality.

TEACHER: Excellent. I'll check back with you in a couple of days to see how it's going.

Notice that the teacher named the strategy for the student when she said, "So you asked yourself the second question: What makes sense for this character?" Also, she asked follow-up questions to get the student to explain his prediction. And finally, when she taught the student a new strategy, she asked him to repeat the plan back to her in order to make sure that the student knew what he was being asked to do and why.

Signal the transition for the share.

Reflect on the Day's Work/Share Our Ideas:

Take a minute to complete you goal sheets. *Give students a minute.* Who exceeded goals today? *Wait for hands.* Who met goals today? *Wait for hands.* Who didn't meet goals? *Wait for hands.*

Well, lots of people are making some pretty amazing predictions. I think instead of hearing your predictions today—because they won't make sense to us, since we're not all reading the same book—can you share something about your process? By process I mean the way you made your predictions. What questions went though your mind? *Call on a few volunteers.*

Did anyone figure out if your predictions were right? *Call on a number of students to share.*

Follow-up:

- *For homework, students should continue to make predictions with evidence. They should also keep track of whether their predictions were correct or needed to be changed. You might have them make a table like this:*

Prediction	Page #	Evidence (with page #)	Correct/not correct

- *To reinforce this lesson, continue modeling making predictions using textual evidence.*

Informal Assessment: Using Multiple Reading Strategies

By the end of this lesson, students will:

- understand that their reading strategies are a "tool box" from which to draw as they read.

Preparation:

1. Review and bring in *I Hadn't Meant to Tell You This* by Jacqueline Woodson (or the book you used in the previous lesson) to read aloud.
2. Display all of the reading charts.

Introduce the Lesson:

Today's lesson is intended as an informal assessment. Using it as such allows you to plan units around reading strategies throughout the year.

As you prepare your read-aloud, think of the different ways readers respond to a variety of texts. You might choose to model a few of the more difficult strategies or the ones your students shy away from. You'll definitely want to refer to the How Good Readers Connect with the Text chart as well as the Personal Connections and Questions to Ask when Making Predictions charts.

We've been practicing the skills and strategies of strong readers for a while now. We know how to make good book choices, how to plan for reading and set goals, how to connect to texts, and how to predict what will happen in our books. Today is a chance for us to practice all of this, which is important because really strong readers do all those things *at the same time* as they read. When good readers get into reading, they think about the book constantly. It just happens. And it's begun to happen for all of you.

Teach the Lesson:

When I read aloud to you today, I'm going to model the connections I make as I read. You'll probably notice that I'm using all the different ways of connecting to texts that we've talked about. As I read, listen for the kinds of connections I'm making. *Read aloud, stopping in places and sharing your connections. After a while, you might want to stop in places and have students share their own connections. Use the following example to help you model the variety of reading strategies:*

TEACHER: I wonder why her mother left? From the information they're giving, she seems happy. I wonder what was going on? *(Example of wondering.)*

Oh, so the main character's name is Marie. I learned that because when her mom is talking to her, she calls her Marie. *(Example of noticing important information about character.)*

This is strange—her mother says there isn't enough air. This seems like a clue about why she left. Maybe she felt suffocated? But I still wonder what was causing her to feel that way. *(Example of asking questions and using evidence to support an idea.)*

I remember riding on the baby swings. I also remember when I got too big for the baby swings and had to move to the big-kid swings. It was scary, but thrilling. *(Example of personal connection.)*

Continue to model your thoughts in this way as you read. Ask your students to share their thoughts as well.

What kinds of connections did you notice I was making? *Take a few responses.* Good. The important thing I wanted you to notice was that I wasn't using just one kind of response. Readers use all kinds of responses at once—they flip-flop between many different strategies. You may have noticed that this already happens for you—you make all kinds of connections as you read. But it might not happen for all of you yet, and if it's not happening for you quite as seamlessly as you'd like, then you'll want to practice making different connections until it just comes naturally.

Transition to Independent Work:

So when you go off and read, use sticky notes to record any responses you have. If you're stuck, look at the charts we have here to remind you of some strategies.

Take a minute now and make a reading goal on your sheet. We're going to be reading for 30 to 35 minutes. You have two minutes to make a goal for yourself and share it with someone near you. If someone's goal doesn't sound realistic to you, help that person set one that makes more sense. *Give students time to make and share goals.*

Okay, reading time. Remember, strong readers have many different kinds of thoughts at once—notice those today. Use your sticky notes to record some of them.

Signal the transition to independent work.

Confer with Students:

During conferences, you might want to ask: How are you using your sticky notes? What kinds of connections are you making as you read? What led you to make that kind of connection? Are you using evidence to support your ideas? Is there any way of connecting to a text that you haven't tried yet? Why? Is there any way of connecting to a text that you'd like to try out today?

If a student is using the same few ways to respond to a text, find out why that is. Has she tried all the different ways to respond, or are there some she feels uncomfortable with? Try to take her outside of her comfort zone for a bit. Model a new way of responding. Ask her to try it as you read.

If a student is reading nonfiction and making connections naturally, you might want to broaden his horizons. Show him how to use sticky notes to record interesting facts. He can try to use them in conversation or incorporate them into his writing.

After your conferences, look back at your records for any patterns you see emerging. Are there certain strategies your students shy away from? Are there areas in which they need more support?

Signal the transition to share time.

Reflect on the Day's Work/Share Our Ideas:

Okay, take out your goal sheets and fill in where you ended and if you met your goal. Show of hands—who met their goal today? *Wait for hands.* Exceeded? *Wait for hands.* Didn't meet? *Wait for hands.* Those of you who are not meeting your goals, we'll meet tomorrow to discuss them and see what's happening.

How did that go? What kinds of responses were people making on their sticky notes today? *Call on a few volunteers.* Are there any ways of responding that you notice you aren't using? *Call on volunteers. Be sure to ask why they think they aren't using certain ways of responding. The information can be helpful in planning future mini-lessons.*

Sounds good! I'm glad to see that so many of you are noticing the connections you have to your books and that you're really using your sticky notes as tools to help you respond to what you're reading.

Follow-up:

- *For homework, students should continue to respond to texts, recording in their reader's notebooks which responses they use and which they do not.*
- *To extend this lesson, model strategies students aren't using or are having difficulty with. It usually takes more than one mini-lesson for students to really understand a strategy.*

Reflecting on Our Thoughts

By the end of this lesson, students will have:
- begun learning how to assess themselves as readers;
- a deeper understanding of the ways they are connecting to texts;
- practiced discussing literature.

Preparation:
1. Review and bring in *I Hadn't Meant to Tell You This* by Jacqueline Woodson (or the book you used in the previous two lessons) to read aloud.
2. Supply copies of the Reading Reflection sheet (see Appendix, p. 158).
3. Create a Reflection Directions chart (see p. 132).

Introduce the Lesson:

Teachers spend a great deal of time thinking about their students—how they're learning, comprehending, writing, and even socializing. Working with students to develop their reflection skills—teaching them to recognize the specific skills and strategies that they're learning as well as the processes by which they learn—helps to create life-long learners.

For the past couple of weeks, we've been working hard to incorporate the strategies of strong readers into our daily reading practice. Today, we're going to continue using sticky notes to record a variety of our responses, but we're also going to take time to reflect on those sticky notes. We're going to investigate what they say about us as readers—the ways we've changed and grown and the work we still need to do to improve our reading abilities.

Teach the Lesson:

As I read aloud today, instead of modeling my thoughts as a reader, I'm going to stop in places and have you share your thoughts with someone near you. This is called a "say something" read-aloud because when I say, "Say something," you'll then start your discussion. While I read, jot down some of your connections, either on sticky notes or in your reader's notebooks, so that when it comes time to discuss what you've heard, you'll have something to refer to. Does that make sense? *Take any questions.*

The following is an example of what a "say something" read-aloud might sound like:

TEACHER: So remember, I'm not going to be modeling my thoughts. You're going to share your thoughts with someone near you when I say, "Say something." I'm going to listen to what you're sharing with each other to see how you're responding to texts, and at times I might ask a few people to share their ideas with the whole class. Ready? Here we go.

"I hadn't meant to tell you this... I stared down at the checkerboard. 'I won't ever tell anybody.'"

After you read a paragraph or two and students have had a chance to make some connections, say, Turn to someone near you and say something to him or her—share a response you have to what you've just heard.

You may overhear a comment like: I wonder what she's not going to tell? *After a minute or two, stop the students. You might find it effective to count down from five, or you might just resume reading, being careful to repeat the last few sentences, so students won't miss any of the story if they're just wrapping up their conversations.*

Finish up your conversations. "I stared down at the checkerboard. 'I won't ever tell anybody.'...

"So I should start at the beginning. And tell the world." Turn to someone near you and say something.

Students turn to each other. The teacher listens to what they're saying, moving around the meeting area to eavesdrop.

Can we stop for a moment? What are some of the things you're noticing? Let's share with the class some of the things you've been sharing with a partner. Can we hear from about three people?

STUDENT A: We were wondering if the secret was about Marie's mom because it seems like it was kind of weird that she left, and she said some strange things. We were wondering if that was what the secret was about.

TEACHER: Can anyone respond to that? Did anyone else have any ideas about that? *Ordinarily, when students share their responses to a reading, they don't speak directly to each other. Having them do so prepares them for discussing literature.*

STUDENT B: Well, we were thinking that it was strange about Marie's mom too.

TEACHER: Okay. Did anyone think the secret was about something else?

The teacher is redirecting the conversation because she's concerned about what Student A is saying. There may not be evidence to support the prediction, and she wants to see if other students can bring that up before mentioning it herself.

STUDENT C: Well, we were thinking that the secret has something to do with her friend Lena—being scared of her dad and stuff. Just because we were thinking of when you read the back and how that connected to what Marie was saying. So, we think the secret has something to do with that. But we also thought the stuff about Marie's mom was weird.

TEACHER: I like how you used evidence for what you were thinking. You remembered the back of the book—you found evidence to support the idea that the secret has to do with Lena and her family. Remember, when you're developing an idea about a book or a character, check your idea against the evidence. Ask yourself if the prediction makes sense based on the evidence you have.

One thing I want to point out to you before we continue is where Marie says, "So I should start at the beginning. And tell the world." This is letting the reader know something. It's letting you know that the rest of the book is going to be a flashback. She tells you she's going to start the story at the beginning. She's going to go back and tell you what's happened from day one. It's as if she's traveling back in time to show you the whole story as it unfolds. When that happens in a book it's called a "flashback." Any questions?

Okay, let's get back to reading and "saying something."

Continue in this way until it's time for independent work.

TEACHER: We've finished our read-aloud for today. Before you begin working independently, I want to talk to you about what you're going to be doing after independent reading. Your reading time is going to be shorter today—we're only going to read for 20 minutes—because I'm asking you to reflect on your sticky notes. We're getting ready to celebrate how we've grown as readers, and as part of that I think it's important to begin thinking more carefully about the ways we respond to our texts on our sticky notes. I'm going to pass out a Reading Reflection sheet.

Here's what you're going to do—I'll remind you of this after independent reading, and I've charted it for you here as well. *Read Reflection Directions to the class.*

Reading Reflection:
Connections and Sticky Notes

1. What do you notice about how you are making connections to your books?

2. Which kinds of connections haven't you tried yet?

3. How does using sticky notes to record your thoughts help you as a reader?

4. What do the connections you record on sticky notes tell you about yourself as a reader?

5. How have you grown as a reader from the first day of class to now?

REFLECTION DIRECTIONS

1. Attach sticky notes from the past two days of reading on the back of your reflection sheet. If you need more room, use a piece of loose-leaf paper.

2. Reread your sticky notes.

3. Answer the questions on the reflection sheet based on what you learn from your sticky notes.

You're going to read for 20 minutes. Then you're going to take the sticky notes you've written over the past two days out of your books and stick them on the back of your reflection sheet. Spread them out so you can read them; don't stack them one on top of the other. If you run out of space, use a piece of loose-leaf paper. Read over your sticky notes. Think about the kinds of responses you're making—are you making a lot of personal connections but not a lot of comments on the author's craft? Then, answer the questions on the front of the sheet.

Go over the questions with students. If they don't understand how to answer, especially questions 3 and 4, help them along. Tell them, Well, you might say something like, "My sticky notes are helping me to be aware of my connections and my thoughts. I can go back and look at them to find evidence to support my ideas. They also let me know how I'm thinking about a character." That kind of thing. Does that help?

Does anyone have any questions? Okay, quickly make a goal for yourself. Share your goal with someone near you. *Give students about one minute to do this.* Go back and start reading. After 20 minutes I'll remind you about your reflection sheets.

Signal the transition to independent work. Watch how students settle in. Make sure they get in 20 minutes of reading time.

Confer with Students:

When students are reflecting on their sticky notes you might help them by asking: What kinds of responses have you been using sticky notes for? Are there any kinds of responses you haven't recorded on sticky notes yet? What do you think your sticky notes say about you as a reader? What do you think your sticky notes do for you as a reader? Are they helping you? Have you noticed any changes in the way you use sticky notes? Did you use sticky notes one way in the beginning but now use them another way? Explain.

Follow-up:

Review your students' Reading Reflection sheets to see what they tell you.

- *If students just don't have many sticky notes, teach a mini-lesson modeling how to use them and when.*
- *Design mini-lessons to address areas of difficulty. If students aren't comparing books (text-to-text responses), model this for them. If they don't make connections to the world around them, model text-to-world connections, and so on.*
- *If students don't see their own improvement, set reading goals with them that will make their strides more apparent. They could make goals about the number of books they want to read or create their own author or genre study.*

Reading Celebrations

Celebrating reading is often overlooked in the Reading Workshop classroom. In Writing Workshop, students can actually hold a finished product, and it will be shared, graded, and published. In fact, it can be published on its own or collected in a class anthology. With reading, things never feel that "finished." However, there are ways to celebrate students' reading accomplishments throughout the year. As you teach your students to become stronger readers, they are growing and changing, not only as readers but also as critical thinkers. These important accomplishments should be acknowledged and celebrated.

Celebrate Independent Reading:

- Have a weekly or bi-monthly book recommendation day. Students bring in books they recently finished and, at the meeting area, present short summaries and rate them. Then, instead of returning those books to the library, students can put them on a "Recommended" shelf. The rating—a set of symbols, such as stars or a thumbs-up—can appear on the front cover on a sticky note with the recommending student's name. This is a wonderful way to launch a community of readers. And students should be encouraged to be honest about their opinions. If they recently read a book they think "stinks," they should let the class know and let them know why. Maybe a classmate has a different opinion.

- Hold favorite or recently finished book walks. Spread the books out on tables in your classroom. The students walk around the room with notebooks, jotting down what they notice *(Most people like fiction books,* or *A lot of people read books by Jerry Spinelli);* questions they have for the person who brought the book in; and lists of books they'd like to read. Then they share their questions and observations. They can then get recommendations and borrow books from each other.

- Teach students how to write quick book reviews. Collect these book reviews and create weekly or bi-monthly newsletters. Set aside class time to hand out, read, and discuss the reviews. These newsletters can also go home to parents and to other classes to recommend books to readers outside of your classroom.

Celebrate Whole-Class Reading Experiences

- After a shared reading experience—when the teacher has read a novel to the class, discussing both reading strategies and the content—students can go off to other classrooms to recommend the book, write letters to the author, write reviews for publication (NCTE's middle-school journal publishes short student reviews, for example), and so on.

- If two classes have read the same book or books by the same author, bring the classes together in small groups or pairs for discussion.

Celebrate Your Reading Lives

- Model your own reading. Keep a reading log of the books you've read in a visible place in the classroom.

- Acknowledge and celebrate students who read on the bus or train—who find time in their lives to read.

- Acknowledge and celebrate students who always have their independent reading books with them—in other classes, for example—and who pull them out to read during any free moment.

- Acknowledge and celebrate students who use facts and information they learn in reading in their writing or conversations. Using what you learn is one of the most beautiful aspects of reading!

Appendix

Conference Sheet

Date: ____________________

Subject: ____________________

RESEARCH — DECIDED — TEACH

Conferred with:	**Discussed:** (How can I help? What's my theory?)	**Possible Mini-Lessons:** (Strategies / Suggestions to address students' questions / Concerns)

Comments/Observations/Plans for Whole-Class Instruction:

Name ______________________________ Date ____________________

Reading Survey

1. How do you feel about reading?

2. How do you feel about yourself as a reader?

3. What is the last good book you read (title, author, when you read it and how you read it—on your own, as part of a class, as a read aloud, etc.)? Why did you like it?

4. What genre (kinds of books) do you like to read? Why?

5. Who is your favorite author?

6. How many books would you say you read last year?

7. How many books do you have at home?

Name ______________________________ Date__________________

Writing Survey

1. What does it mean to be a writer?

2. Do you consider yourself a writer? If no, why not? If yes, why?

3. Do you have a writer's notebook? If so, what kinds of writing do you gather in there? If not, what do you imagine a writer's notebook might look like?

4. Do you have a favorite writing genre?

5. Have you been a successful writer in the past? Do you feel like writing has always been a struggle for you? Explain either answer fully.

Notebook Rubric

	1 below standards	2 approaching standards	3 meeting standards	4 exceeds standards
Amount: Do I have the right number of entries? Did I write at least full page per entry?				
Use: Do I have different kinds of entries? Have I taken notes on mini-lessons?				
Thoughtfulness: Did I spend time on my entries?				
Presentation: Do I have the right headings? Are my entries dated?				

	1	2	3	4
Amount: Do I have the right number of entries? Did I write at least full page per entry?				
Use: Do I have different kinds of entries? Have I taken notes on mini-lessons?				
Thoughtfulness: Did I spend time on my entries?				
Presentation: Do I have the right headings? Are my entries dated?				

Homework

I think homework is unfair. After a really long day at school, Teenagers just want to go home, watch some television and relax. We go to school from 8:30 a.m. to 3:00 p.m. That is most of our day! We study hard in school only to come home to more studying.

I also think homework makes no sense. What if there is no one at home to help you with homework? What if you didn't understand it in school and still don't understand it at home? Some parents work late and some don't speak English. How can they help us?

Kids deserve a break. We have other things that interest us. Many of us have dance classes after school and basketball games, swimming meets and other extracurricular activities to attend. Why do we have to give up doing what we love to extend the learning day into our personal lives?

Teachers put too much pressure on kids. Let us just be young while we have the chance. Let up on the homework. Please!!!!!

Name ______________________________ Date__________________

Writing Reflection

1. What kinds of entries did you write in your notebook? (list the different kinds)

2. Do any topics appear in your notebook that you have written about before, maybe in another class or for another project? If so, list the topic or topics.

3. Are there any topics in your notebook that you never wrote about before? If so, list the topic or topics.

4. Which entry excites or puzzles or troubles or grabs you most? Why?

5. Which entries did you spend the most time working on?

6. Which entries did you spend the least time working on?

7. Which entries would you share with the class? Why?

8. Are there any entries that are similar? Do you write about a memory a few times in your notebook? Do you write about one topic over and over again? Do you write about one person a lot?

9. Are there any sentences that you wrote that stand out from the rest? Could you add more to these sentences to make new writing?

10. Remember, you are not choosing a favorite entry. You are choosing a topic to write about further. You are choosing an idea. Right now choose two possible topic ideas from your notebook and discuss why you might choose them to develop in longer pieces of writing.

Gracelynn C.W.
10-16

Draft 1
How The Kids On My Block Act!

The Kids on my block act really strange! They go to School like me and play outside like me, but they are from a different back rounds than me and have different cultures! Some of them think they are in a gang, and some of them are in a gang! I think they have made the wrong desision to hang out with kids that are trouble! Now, Since they started to hanging out with them, they have become ~~even bigger troue~~ trouble makers!

Even though some kids on my block act that way,

Draft 1, Page 2

there are still a couple of kids who have a lot in comen with me. There names are Bryant, Hermitas, and a lot more!

I hope I never become like them, and continue to stay away from them!!!!!!!!

Gracelynn
10-23

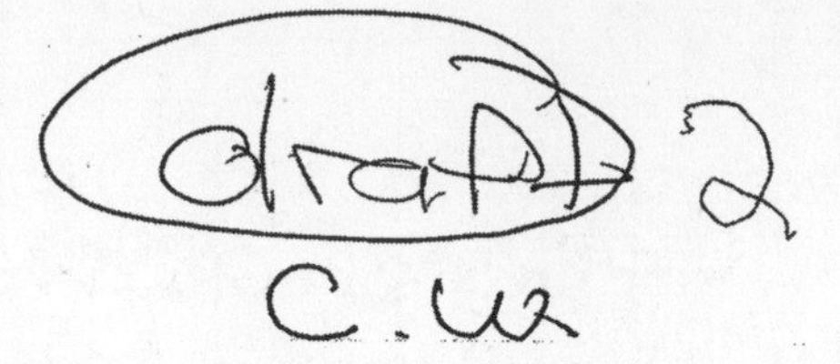

How The kids On My Block Act!

(P.1) They were hanging out on the corner of the street with there baggy close and there bad attitude! There really strange Even though they go to school like me, and go outside to hang out like me, They want to be in a gang! Yes A Gang! Why would somebody want to be a bad person? I know I wouldn't!!!! (P.2) I think they have made the wrong decision! Before they have started to hang out with them, they were good kids. But when they started hanging out with them they become trouble makers too!

(P 3) Even though that some kids on my block act that ways some kids are really nice! There names are Bryant, Hermites, and a lot more!

I hope I never become the way that those kids are!

Heading

How The Kids On My Block Act!

They were hanging out on the corner of the street with their baggy close and there bad attitude! them really strange. Even though they go to school like me and hang with their friends like me, they are in a gang! Who would want to be in a gang? Why would someone want to be a bad person? I know I wouldn't!

Anyway I think that they have made the wrong decision when they joined that gang! Before they had

Draft 3, Page 2

joined that gang, they had a lot in common with me! Now, They don't have anything in common with me! !!!!!!!!!!!!!!!!!!!!!!!!!!!!!!!! Now they are just trouble!!!

Even though they are like that, sp. there their are still kids that are sp. differen different, and don't act that way. sp. There Their names are Hermidas, and Bryant.

I hope I never start acting like that!

Sample of Student's Published Work

How The Kids On My Block Act

They were hanging out at the corner of the street with their baggy clothes and their bad attitude. They're really weird. Even though they go to school like me, and hang out with their friends like me, they are in a gang. Why would someone want to be in a gang? Why would someone want to be a bad person?

I know I wouldn't.

I think that they made the wrong decision when they joined that gang. Before they joined that gang, they were good kids. They weren't trouble makers, and they had a lot in common with me. Now they have nothing in common with me. Now they are just trouble.

My parents and friends always tell me to stay away from those people. They also tell me to have nothing to do with them. Even if they didn't tell me that, I would still stay away from them because I know they're trouble.

Even though they act like that, there are still kids on my block that don't act like that. Their names are Hermitas, and Bryant. They are different. They made the right decision. They know what's right and wrong. And they know who to hang out with. Why can't everybody know what's right and wrong? Why can't the world be different? I wish those gangsters would just realize that they have made the wrong decision. I wish they would just stand up to there friends and tell them its wrong.

I hope I never become like them.

Five Kinds of Leads

(Remember: The lead should grab your reader's attention.)

1. Action—The reader is immediately drawn into the action of the story.

I heard a loud crash, my little brother screamed, and I started running. When I got to the backyard, blood was everywhere and Michael was sitting holding his knee, crying. Pieces of broken bottle lay in the blood pooling around him. I began to panic.

2. Dialogue—The text begins with one or more people speaking.

"Jason! Jason, help me!"

I ran out the kitchen door to the backyard, where my bother was playing. When I got there, I knew it was bad.

"Are you…? Are you…"

That was all I could say. Nothing else would come out of my mouth.

3. Setting—This traditional beginning describes time and place.

One Saturday night during the summer, my parents decided to go to a movie. I was in charge of my little brother Michael, and I was in a bad mood. I didn't want to baby-sit on Saturday night. Michael was much younger than I and really annoying. He always got into my stuff and asked too many questions while I watched television.

4. One-Sentence Wonders—The opening paragraph is only one sentence long, and it's provocative.

I will never forgive myself for what happened to Michael.

5. Reflection—The narrator examines the subject, describing thoughts and feelings.

I never appreciated my little brother Michael. I thought he was annoying, a nuisance, a burden. But that horrible night I learned how important he is to me. I realized I would do anything for Michael. Anything.

Visiting—Draft #1

I woke up at about 5am when my alarm clock rang. Beep. Beep. I didn't want to get up I was so tired. But I knew today was my big day to go visit my dad in Delaware. I got up and went to the kitchen and ate breakfast with my mom. I ate some cereal and then got dressed. When I was ready my mom said "come on Benny we are gonna be late". So, we left and we took the train to the bus station. Their were many people in the train station so many I felt trapped. I waited with my mom for the bus and then kissed her goodbye. I couldn't wait to visit my Dad in Delaware. The bus was crowded and I listened to my walkman the whole way. It was a long ride. I ate the lunch my mom packed for me. I ate a sandwich and soda and chips. I looked out the window and saw lots of cars and big green signs. We went over a very big, wide bridge. I was sad because I already missed my mom.

The bus finally got to Delaware and when I got off the bus I saw my aunt and two cousins waiting for me. I hugged my aunt and said hi to my cousins and then we got in her car and drove to my dad's house. I gave my dad a hug and then we went out to eat to Red Lobster. The next day my aunt and two cousins took me to the movies and then I slept at her house for a slumber party.

We had so much fun. I really loved being in Delaware with my dad. When I came home I was happy to see my mom but sad to leave my dad and aunt.

Dog Care

If you have a dog. Dogs need to be taken good care of. They need to be washed a lot and fed all the time. Dogs need to be walked and need to have a place to play and a place to sleep. They need a comfortable place to lay down. you have to always watch out for your dog and make sure it don't get hit by a car. Also when you have a dog you take the dog to a animal doctor called a veterinarian. You should love your pet and give it a good home and brush his fur everyday so that he doesn't shed too much in the house. Also if you have little kids in your house you should watch out for the dog could bite the little kids. If you play too rough. Sometimes, people sneeze from dogs and then you have to give them away. But not if you brush the dog everyday then you can stop him from shedding too much. I have a dog and I love him very much and I take good care of him. Do you take care of your dog?

Writing in Paragraphs

SAMPLE 1

When I grow up I want to be a veterinarian. A veterinarian is an animal doctor. I love animals and that is why I want to help take care of them when I am older. I know you have to go to school for a long time to be an animal doctor. You have to have a degree from high school, college and veterinary school. You also need to have high grades and intern in an animal hospital before you can own your own practice. When I own my practice, it will be in Brooklyn because that is where I am from. There are a lot of animals that need love in Brooklyn like stray cats and dogs. I want to help give these lost animals check ups and homes. I will never charge a fee for an animal brought in from the street without a home. Whoever brings those animals in should be thanked not charged. My dog is named Jake and I love him. He is a black mixed Labrador and he is the reason I decided to become a Vet.

SAMPLE 2

When mama got home from work, she was exhausted. I asked her, "Mama, can I have money for my school trip?" Mama hardly looked at me as she mumbled to herself and threw her tired body onto the couch. "Baby, rub mama's feet, then we'll talk money." I hated rubbing her feet. I was the only one in the house who ever did it. Would Johnny? My brother was too wrapped up in himself and Papa didn't get home until after bedtime. Mama worked hard on her feet all day at a grocery store. I felt bad asking her for money and I felt bad that she had hurt feet. As I sat on the floor, I massaged her feet as she told me about her day. "Mr. Jones really did it today. He was so rude to me in front of a customer." I grew red with anger. "What did he say to you; mama?" I carefully worked my thumbs into her soles. Mama answered, "He told me I was lazy and worked too slowly." Mama looked sad. I knew she was one of his best workers but when Mr. Jones was in a bad mood he took it out on Mama. Papa always tells her to quit, "Sandra, quit that job, we'll make do." But Mama won't quit. She knows how hard Papa works already. "I have a growing girl who needs things," Mama always responds. Mama wanted me to have all that she didn't.

Name ______________________________

Writing Evaluation

Standard	Above Standard	Meets Standard	Approaching Standard	Below Standard
Student planned the first draft by using an outline or a map in the writer's notebook.				
Student created a first draft by using writing from a variety of entries, not just one.				
Student wrote five different leads before choosing one that catches the reader's attention.				
Student was able to add writing to the draft that was missing and delete writing that did not belong.				
Student work written in paragraph form.				
Student work has been checked for spelling errors.				

KEY Above standard = 4 points
Meets standard = 3 points
Approaching standard = 2 points
Below standard = 1 point

Class ____________________ Name ________________________________

Reading Record

Title	Author	Genre	Date Started	Date Abandoned	Date Finished	Rating (1–10)

Name ____________________________________

Daily Reading Goals

Title	Date	Goal	Time Start	Page Start	Time End	Page End	Goal Reached

Reading Reflection: Connections and Sticky Notes

1. What do you notice about how you are making connections to your books?

2. Which kinds of connections haven't you tried yet?

3. How does using sticky notes to record your thoughts help you as a reader?

4. What do the connections you record on sticky notes tell you about yourself as a reader?

5. How have you grown as a reader from the first day of class to now?

Professional Book List

For overviews of Reading and Writing Workshop structure:

Atwell, Nancie (1998). *In the Middle.* Portsmouth, NH: Heinemann.

Calkins, Lucy. (2001). *The Art of Teaching Reading.* New York: Addison Wesley.

Calkins, Lucy. (1994). *The Art of Teaching Writing.* Portsmouth, NH: Heinemann.

Calkins, Lucy. (1990). *Living Between the Lines.* Portsmouth, NH: Heinemann.

Specifics of Reading and Writing Workshop:

Allen, Janet. (2001). *Yellow Brick Roads.* Portland, ME: Stenhouse.

Anderson, Carl. (2000). *How's It Going?* Portsmouth, NH: Heinemann.

Benedict, Susan and Lenore Carlisle. (1992). *Beyond Words.* Portsmouth, NH: Heinemann.

Bomer, Randy. (1995). *Time for Meaning.* Portsmouth, NH: Heinemann.

Fletcher, Ralph and Joann Portalupi. (1998). *Craft Lessons.* Portland, ME: Stenhouse.

Fletcher, Ralph. (1996). *A Writer's Notebook.* New York: HarperTrophy.

Keene, Ellin Oliver and Susan Zimmerman. (1997). *Mosaic of Thought.* Portsmouth, NH: Heinemann.

Harvey, Stephanie. (1998). *Nonfiction Matters.* Portland, ME: Stenhouse.

Harvey, Stephanie and Anne Goudvis. (2000). *Strategies That Work.* Portland, ME: Stenhouse.

Heard, Georgia. (1995). *Writing Toward Home.* Portsmouth, NH: Heinemann.

Macrorie, Ken. (1998). *The I-Search Paper.* Portsmouth, NH: Boynton/Cook.

Portalupi, Joann and Ralph Fletcher. (2001). *Nonfiction Craft Lessons.* Portland, ME: Stenhouse.

Ray, Katie Wood. (1999). *Wondrous Words.* Urbana, IL: NCTE.

Ray, Katie Wood. (2001). *The Writing Workshop.* Urbana, IL: NCTE.

Robb, Laura. (2000). *Teaching Reading in Middle School.* New York: Scholastic.

Smith, Frank. (1978). *Reading Without Nonsense.* New York: Teachers College Press.

Wilde, Sandra. (2000). *Miscue Analysis Made Easy.* Portsmouth, NH: Heinemann.

Wilde, Sandra. (1997). *What's a Schwa Sound, Anyway?* Portsmouth, NH: Heinemann.

Theoretical Reading/Constructivist Philosophy:

Delpit, Lisa. (1996). *Other People's Children.* New York: New Press.

Dewy, John. (1997). *Democracy in Education.* New York: Free Press.

Friere, Paulo. (2000). *Pedagogy of the Oppressed.* New York: Continuum.

hooks, bell. (1994). *Teaching to Transgress.* New York: Routledge.

Horton, Myles and Paulo Friere. (1991). *We Make the Road by Walking.* Philadelphia, PA: Temple University Press.

Pradl, Gordon. (1996). *Literature for Democracy.* Portsmouth, NH: Boynton/Cook.

Rosenblatt, Louise. (1983). *Literature as Exploration,* 4th ed. New York: The Modern Language Association of America.

Vygotsky, Lev. (1986). *Thought and Language,* Revised Edition. Boston, MA: MIT Press.

Testing:

Calkins, Lucy, Kate Montgomery, Donna Santman, and Beverly Falk. (1999). *A Teacher's Guide to Standardized Reading Tests.* Portsmouth, NH: Heinemann.